ESCANTA

A JAMES THOMAS NOVEL

BROOKE SIVENDRA

DEDICATION

This book is dedicated to the Sivendra family.
Thank you for welcoming me into your family.
Your love and kindness is unparalleled.

PROLOGUE

Every man had a purpose in life.

For some, it was family.

For others, it was high-powered careers, fast cars, and beautiful women.

For James Thomas, it was to survive.

His hand was steady as he pushed the pistol into his new friend's mouth.

"You're not a fast learner, are you?" James asked, the gaze of his black eyes gouging at the man's soul.

Having pulled his friend out of the torture tank, the man sat, tied up to a metal chair, and water dripped off his clothes, forming a puddle at his feet.

His victim responded with a string of words muffled by the Glock stuffed in his mouth. James withdrew the weapon, pressing it against the man's temple instead.

"Say again," James said.

The man panted, drawing in deep, heaving breaths. "Please, you don't understand what they will do to me. These aren't men, they're animals. They have no conscience, no soul. The things they do to people . . . things you can't possibly imagine. If I tell you, you have to protect me."

James shook his head slowly. "I'm not making a deal. And believe me, if you don't tell me, you will wish that they were punishing you instead. If you think you know me, think again—you have no idea what I'm capable of. Everything you have seen over the past few years —every piece of information you have collected about me—it is just a fragment of who I am. The life I live now is very different from my past, and I miss my old life—I miss terrorizing the fucked-up men of humanity. The monotony in my paper-pushing day job makes me hungry for action, and when an opportunity like this comes along," James said, nodding his head to his guest, "I get to unleash my full set of skills. And you should understand that the torture tank was just a warm-up—I personally prefer body mutilation, and I'm *very* good at it. So think about this carefully, because you still have a choice. You can tell me who sent you, or I will take my scalpel to your head and peel back your face. Which is it going to be?"

The man closed his eyes, his teeth crunching against each other so violently James thought he heard one crack.

With his free hand, he pulled a knife from his back pocket and slammed it into the man's thigh. He howled in agony.

"I'm running out of patience. Who sent you?" James's voice was menacing, the kind of voice that ran shivers up your spine. A voice he'd perfected through thousands of interrogations.

The man cursed. "I don't know his name. We call him Faber, but that's it, that's all I know."

"You need to give me more information than that," James said, holding a second knife over the man's other thigh.

"The group, the organization . . ." The man's voice cracked as tears dropped from his eyes. "It's called Escanta. They have been hunting you for years. That's all I know, I swear, I don't know who's in charge, who Faber reports to."

James looked into the man's pleading eyes.

"I believe you," James said and pulled the trigger.

1

MAK ASHWOOD

Death is but an illusion, as you will soon see.

Mak's hands trembled as she read the note. She looked up, alert, her pulse rapid as her eyes scanned her hotel room. Her skin prickled, like she was being watched, but there was no one there. She'd rushed in from breakfast to pick up her bags, when she'd found the scroll sitting atop the large bed. The words were written on delicate white paper, rolled up and secured with a red ribbon.

Her eyes scanned the room again, but she was alone. How did the scroll get into her room? Was the hotel responsible for the breach? Or was it someone else?

She was working on a big case, and that meant potential enemies. Prosecuting the head of the mob for a triple murder definitely didn't win you any friends.

Mak swallowed the lump in her throat, threw the scroll in her carry-on, and grabbed her bags. The room felt wrong now; the air felt cold and the energy was icky, like death itself had invaded and tainted every molecule.

Mak closed the door behind her and hurried to the elevator. She put on a brave face, in the event that someone was watching her. She had no doubt the scroll had been intended to rattle her, and she wouldn't give them the satisfaction of knowing it had turned her blood to ice. When the elevator doors opened, she was grateful to see the carriage was crowded—there was safety in numbers—and exhaled a shaky breath.

She had hired a personal bodyguard as the case had heated up and the trial was about to begin, however, they usually only accompanied her from her home to the office or the courthouse. She hadn't thought it necessary to have her bodyguard accompany her on the short, unplanned trip.

Mak had received the telephone call last weekend—the parents of one of her best friends from high school had been killed in a car accident. Mak had dropped everything, even though she was preparing for the trial of her life, to fly to London and be with her friend for the funeral. It had been an exhausting and utterly draining forty-eight hours in London, but on the positive side she'd been able to spend some time with a friend she hadn't seen in four years, and such was life—it could be cruel, and, at the same time, it could be beautiful.

But maybe Mak should've brought security with her. Her friend's family had a high profile in London, and she'd known there would be security at the funeral, but maybe she had underestimated the risks. Or maybe this was just a harmless threat to rile her up. It was a successful stunt, if that had indeed been their objective.

The elevator doors opened and Mak wheeled her luggage to the express check-out box. She considered bringing the security breach to the hotel's attention, but if they questioned her for more than five minutes, which had to be expected, she would miss her flight back to New York. No, she would have her security deal with it—she was paying him enough, after all.

Mak used the time in the car to check her emails. Her eyes scanned them, and she spotted one from Maya, her sister, which would be far from urgent but she opened it anyway as a means to steady herself.

To: Makaela Ashwood
From: Maya Ashwood
Subject: Tonight

Mak,

I picked up your gown from the dry cleaner and dropped it off at your apartment so it's ready for you when you get home from the airport. I'll meet you at the party because I don't want to be late. Can't wait to have a champs!

XO

Mak smiled; she was looking forward to a night out. She needed a drink after the intensity of the last few days, and she needed a break from the reality of her career. It wasn't a nine-to-five job, and it wasn't a matter of just doing a good job—justice lay in her hands and grieving families depended on her success.

And she couldn't wait to see Maya. Maya had always been her sidekick, even though they were just two of six siblings. They were very close, perhaps because of the small age difference of one year between them, but they were opposites in every other way. Mak's natural blond hair and sea-blue eyes were in contrast to Maya's brunette hair and brown eyes. Their personalities were also dichotomous—Maya had a bohemian flair and traveled the world for her interior design career, while Mak flirted with the ugly side of life as a criminal prosecutor. Regardless, their bond was tight, and they had remained close despite Maya never being in one country for longer than a few weeks at a time.

Mak fired back a quick email response, thanking Maya for organizing her gown, and then turned her attention to more important matters. The time passed quickly but when she checked her watch she realized she'd been in the car much longer than she'd allowed for. As soon as the car pulled to a stop, Mak threw some cash at the driver and ran into the airport.

The final check-in call was being announced as Mak rushed up to the counter, skipping the queue and cursing London's traffic. The window had been tight as it was, and the traffic had been gridlocked today.

"Where to, ma'am?" the lady greeted her.

"New York," Mak said, handing over her passport.

The lady's fingers typed quickly, rapidly entering data into the computer. "Just in the nick of time, ma'am," she said, handing Mak her boarding pass.

"Thank you," Mak said graciously.

Juggling her carry-on and her handbag, she picked up her passport and boarding pass and made her way through the arduous security toward the gate. She was the last to board.

"Have a great flight," a gentleman said as he scanned her boarding pass.

Mak hurried onto the plane, her eyes running across the overhead compartments, scanning the numbers until she found her seat. 6B. Mak didn't normally fly business class but given the long travel times, the short duration of the trip, and the fact that she needed to catch up on some work, she'd afforded herself the luxury and she didn't regret it one bit—it was worth every damn penny.

Mak quickly pulled her laptop and cell phone from her carry-on and stuffed her bags in the overhead cabinet. She paused when her skin tingled; she had that innate sense she was being watched again. She looked over her fellow passengers, stopping on a pair of mysterious, black eyes. Her heart lurched and stumbled over itself—there was something different about him: a sense of danger that even his handsome face couldn't disguise. Was it a coincidence that he was on her flight? Or was he intentionally on her flight? *How hard would it be to find out my flight details?* Mak asked herself. *Not very.* Her eyes scanned over the other passengers, but no one else seemed to be paying attention to either of them. She looked back to the mystery man and their eyes connected again. *Oh shit.*

"Excuse me, you need to take your seat now," the flight attendant said, pulling Mak's attention from the man three rows behind her.

"Sorry, of course," Mak said, sitting down. Her heart was

pounding wildly again. *Who is he?* Mak stuffed her laptop into the chair storage and leaned forward, resting her face in her hands. First the scroll and now the man seated behind her—it was too much, and something definitely didn't feel right.

"Excuse me, Miss, are you not feeling well?"

The attendant was back again and the last thing Mak wanted was to create a scene. She responded quickly, "I'm fine, thank you, just tired."

The attendant gave her a beautiful smile. "Okay, please let me know if you need anything during the flight."

Mak made a concerted effort to appear relaxed as she leaned back in her seat. Her nerves were frayed, and she wanted to get off this flight, but it was too late now. She had to try and relax and think about an exit plan because she might be safe now, but what about when they disembarked the aircraft? Mak thought it through and could only come up with one plan: get to the waiting security car—fast.

Mak took several deep breaths, glad that her chair concealed her somewhat from the mysterious man. It could be nothing; she could be making it all up in her head. But if it was nothing, why was he looking at her like that? It wasn't a look like he was hitting on her, definitely not. It was like she was a mystery to him, and Mak had no logical explanation except that he might be involved in the security breach.

It doesn't make sense, though. If someone wanted to hurt her, and they knew she was traveling on this flight, it would've been better to attempt something before she left London or once she arrived in New York. What good would it do to have someone follow her on the plane? If they knew her flight details, they knew where she was land- ing, and it wasn't like she was going to jump off the plane mid-flight.

The plane began to taxi toward the runway, and Mak placed her hands on the armrests. She had a moderate fear of flying, and takeoff was her least favorite part of the experience. She closed her eyes, trying to calm her anxious mind and let her head drop back against the headrest. But as the plane sped up, so did her anxiety. Her fingers wrapped around the armrests, and she held her breath as the front wheels came up. Only once the plane had finished climbing did she pry her hands away and move them into her lap.

Wanting to distract herself, Mak pulled her laptop from the seat compartment and fired it up. If there was one way she'd learned to deal with her aviation-related anxiety, other than taking a sleeping pill, it was to work. She opened her email program and finished responding to those she hadn't gotten to in the car.

Mak had made a name for herself quickly, taking on high-risk cases, and so far it was a strategy that had paid off—in terms of career success at least. State prosecutors earned peanuts compared to private lawyers, but Mak didn't care so much about the money as long as she had enough to live comfortably in New York City.

But the case she was currently working on, the triple murder, was a difficult case, and the odds were stacked against her. She had faith, though, and believed in herself. She could do it. She had to—for the families of the victims and to prevent a murderer from walking free and hurting another living soul.

Mak was sending the last email when the mysterious man from 9C walked past her, toward the front of the plane. She raised her eyes just enough to observe him. He was tall, over six-foot—she guessed—and well built. He was not bulky like a bodybuilder, but he looked strong. And he walked with a confident ease—long, purposeful strides—but Mak couldn't imagine where he was going other than the bathroom.

When he disappeared behind the curtain, Mak released the breath she had been subconsciously holding. He was certainly attractive, and she noted she hadn't been the only one watching him walk by. But it wasn't just the olive skin, dark eyes, and shaved head that made him mysterious. It was something else, something she couldn't put her finger on. It was unsettling, and again she wished she could get off the airplane before he returned to his seat. *Far too late, Mak.*

Her email alert captured her focus once more, and she was grateful for the distraction. She turned her eyes from the aisle and back to her screen. It was an email from her assistant, containing a routine update—certainly nothing sufficient to hold her attention at the present moment. It had taken her three hours of email to suppress the anxiety she'd felt upon boarding the plane, and within seconds the mystery-man had resurrected it.

Mak looked up at the restroom signs now and realized they were all green. If he wasn't in the bathroom, where was he? And what could he possibly be doing?

Five minutes passed, and she felt his eyes before she heard him. Her blood spiked with adrenaline, and when she looked up, he was looking directly at her. His expression was as unreadable as it had been the first time their eyes locked. His eyes were like black, bottomless holes but the gaze they generated was commanding. Her chest constricted, and she broke eye-contact and looked at her laptop.

As he passed her row she smelled a fine trace of cologne—a masculine, fresh note with a hint of cinnamon that, although faint, insulted her senses. Senses that were already heightened by the alert state of her mind. *At least if he attacks me from behind I'll know who it is.*

Mak closed her eyes. Twice he had made eye-contact with her, and twice he'd made no effort to hide it. Her unease made it more difficult to rationally analyze the situation and his behavior. She mentally profiled him, like she did for a witness or defendant, but she still couldn't figure him out. She was usually good at reading people, and that's probably why she was good at what she did—she knew when the defendants were lying and when to push them. But she read nothing from him. Nothing.

The plane bounced unexpectedly and Mak grabbed the armrests. It quickly settled again and Mak said a quiet thank you—she did not need a bout of turbulence to send her over the edge. She released the in-flight television remote from the chair and turned on the flight path.

Seven hours to go.

Mak questioned if she'd have had the same reaction to him if the scroll hadn't already set off her nerves. Was her mind spinning so wildly out of control that she'd built it all up in her head? None of the other passengers seemed fazed by his presence. None of them were cowering in their seats as he walked past. Only her. But then she hadn't seen him giving any of the other passengers the same look he gave her, either.

Her mind was like a centrifuge, spinning her thoughts around and around. She wished she had been seated in a row behind him so she could watch him, keep tabs on him. If he was after her, she wasn't going to make it easy for him.

I wonder if that's how Eric felt? Eric was her husband—her husband who had disappeared thirteen years ago.

Her husband's disappearance was something she had come to accept over the years. At first, she'd been devastated and concerned. But every night he hadn't come home the worry and anxiety had faded, until it ceased to exist—Mak no longer expected him to return. She'd never been able to find out what had happened to him, but she knew him and his tenacity, and if he met with foul play, he wouldn't have made it easy to take him or to hurt him.

Mak and her husband had married young, at the tender age of twenty-two, and, if she were being honest, it was unlikely their marriage would have lasted even if he hadn't gone missing. They were two very ambitious people who put their own needs first. Always. They both wanted success, which was probably why they had connected in the first place, but ultimately that drive would've destroyed them. Anyone who'd been married for longer than five minutes will tell you that dedicating all of your time to your career, and none to your spouse, is not a good recipe for a long and happy marriage.

Mak still clearly remembered the night he went missing, as uneventful as it had seemed at the time. She'd been up late studying for a law exam when he called, saying he'd be home within the hour. It was nothing out of the ordinary that he had been out late, since he was often at some networking event or another, and she'd barely responded, more irritated than anything that he'd disrupted her study just to tell her he'd be home soon. But four hours later when she'd looked up from the textbooks her head had been buried in, he still wasn't home. And he hadn't walked in the door since.

Some days, like today, Mak thought about her husband, and other days he was completely absent from her thoughts. She had initially hired a private investigator to look for him, after the police had come up with nothing, but they, too, proved fruitless and a waste of money. Eventually, after years without a single answer, she'd given up and moved on with her life. She still wished she knew what had happened to him, though. And she wished she had a body to bury and a chance to say goodbye.

But life wasn't going to give her that.

2

JAMES THOMAS

"Samuel," James said, deliberately slowing down to ensure he stayed six paces behind the petite blonde who had kept him awake all flight. He'd intended to sleep, as he'd done so little of it lately, but she'd been an unexpected distraction. And an unwelcome one. "Anything to report?"

"No, you need to give me more time, James," Samuel replied.

James didn't want to give him more time—he wanted answers, and he wanted them now. He wanted to know who Escanta was, and why they were hunting him.

But he'd also worked with Samuel for a long time, and he knew the lack of information wasn't from a lack of trying. James masked his frustration, which he knew better than to take out on Samuel, particularly given his next request.

"Okay. Also, I need you to run a report on a woman named Makaela Ashwood. She was sitting in seat 6B on my flight. Send it to my phone when you're done."

James dropped farther behind when Makaela didn't turn at the exit to the baggage carousel, but instead continued toward the airport exit. *She wasn't in London long, then, if she'd only taken a carry-on.* He knew she was American, based on the accent he'd picked up when she was talking to the flight attendant, so chances were she lived in New York.

"Ah, sure. But why?" Samuel asked.

James didn't have the answer, or at least a suitable answer. She'd captured his attention from the moment she walked onto the plane. She was stunning with small features and plush lips. But the longer he observed her the more he saw the contradictions in her appearance versus her personality. He'd been watching her, trying to work out why she had him so intrigued, when she'd turned to face him. She met his gaze and didn't back down—not even from the look he was giving her. It wasn't a look intending to scare her, but nor was it a look inviting her to flirt with him. He couldn't remember being instantly so attracted to a woman, which in equal parts both fascinated and concerned him. Perhaps recent events had affected him more than he realized. Regardless, he wanted to know more about her, even if he intended to do nothing with the information.

"I'm not sure yet," James said elusively.

Samuel paused but didn't press further. "Well, when do you want this? I can only do so much," he said, and James could hear him typing as he spoke.

Samuel was a brilliant computer hacker, and over the years they had grown so close that James now considered Samuel family. And he was one of only three people James completely trusted.

"Run it now; it shouldn't take too long, and then get back to Escanta. I want to know what this organization is," James said, moving into the taxi queue with no intention of catching a cab. He was still watching her and everyone around them—he was always alert, his eyes always darting from point to point. With his past, everything that moved was a potential threat.

"Right, I'll send it through when it's done," Samuel said. "By the way, how did you get her name?"

James grinned. "Let's just say the attendants shouldn't leave their paperwork lying around."

Samuel laughed. "I see. I'll get back to you shortly," he said before ending the call.

James slid his phone into his pocket.

Makaela looked over her shoulder, as if looking for a shadow. She'd done it several times, and she'd looked uneasy on the flight. *Why is she so anxious? What does she have to fear?* A black car pulled up and a man, who was not the driver, stepped out and ushered her into the car. *Security.* James memorized the number plate as it drove off and then sent it to Samuel. *Why does Makaela Ashwood need security?*

James ducked out of the taxi line and walked toward the parking lot, where a *Thomas Security* car was waiting for him. He looked over his own shoulder now, checking for any shadows, but he was safe for the moment. London had been an unexpected trip, and one he wished he hadn't had to take. But the thing about your past is that it's never far behind you, and it always catches up with you.

James had been tying up some loose ends for a client in Spain when he noticed he had a shadow other than his own. It happened in a restaurant. He noticed a pair of eyes looking at him one too many times and his sixth-sense told him not to ignore it. James had a friendly chat with the man in the bathroom, left with the man's phone, and then put Samuel to work. Three hours later he was on a flight to London.

James reversed out of the parking bay and exited the lot, driving directly to Thomas Security—his company's headquarters and his residence. Thomas Security was a purpose-built building and was the safest place on earth for him and Deacon, his brother, Samuel, and Cami. They had everything they needed in one building, and it was riddled with escape routes. They hadn't had to use them yet, and hopefully they never would.

When James pulled into the company parking lot he checked his phone: nothing from Samuel. He grabbed his overnight bag, slung it over his shoulder, and took the elevator up to his apartment. He went through the motions of unlocking his door—a series of security passes that included fingerprint and retina matches—and then walked into a silent, dark foyer. The curtains were drawn, as they always were, and his apartment looked like a showroom. There was nothing personal—no photographs, no travel mementos, and no family heirlooms. There was no point collecting possessions when you might need to disappear and leave it all behind. And he had no memories, let alone heirlooms, of his family. One of Thomas Security's best-kept secrets was that the two brothers who ran it were not really brothers at all—at least not biologically. But they had become brothers in every other sense, and James thought of Deacon as his brother, as family.

James dropped his bag onto the floor of his bedroom and walked to his en-suite. He stripped off his clothes and stepped underneath the shower for only a few minutes. He had to be somewhere, and he was already late.

James threw the towel over his head, drying his shaved scalp and the rest of his body, and then hung it up, walking naked to his bedroom. He dressed in a black suit and debated whether he should wear a bow tie or a necktie. He settled on a necktie, knotted it, and then checked his phone again: still no report.

He ran a finger along his brow in frustration. He was itching to call Samuel and find out why it was taking so long, but Samuel didn't take well to being pestered—James knew this from experience. He also knew interrupting him constantly was counterproductive. But what could be taking so long? Samuel could create a basic security report in minutes—personal details, bank accounts, employment history, relationship history—it was all readily accessible if you knew where to look and had access to the files.

James heard his apartment door open, but he didn't panic. There were only four people with a code to his apartment, and for anyone else, it was virtually impassable. James met Cami in the hallway.

"You scrub up nicely," Cami said. She was one of his most valuable employees, and one of his only true friends, along with Samuel and Deacon. She pushed a wrapped gift into his hands and adjusted his tie. He shooed her away.

"What's this?" James asked, assessing the gift.

"A present for Zahra and Jayce. You can't turn up to an engagement party without a gift. You do realize that, don't you?"

James rolled his eyes and walked toward his kitchen. Cami followed him.

"What did you buy?" James asked. It was surprisingly heavy, and he set it on the kitchen island while he poured himself a glass of juice. He held up the container but Cami shook her head, indicating she didn't want one.

"It's a gift from Thomas Security, as such. I bought a beautiful album. It even has a glass front, and I printed a collection of photographs from our surveillance."

James blinked in surprise. It was a thoughtful gift, even if a little unusual. Zahra Foster and Jayce Tohmatsu were clients of Thomas Security, and their case had been one of the most difficult James had ever worked on—primarily because there were so many unknown factors, and so many elements of their past that it had been nearly impossible to know who and what they were dealing with. He hoped to never see a case like that again. They were still clients of Thomas Security, but their security had been dramatically downgraded. James hoped it stayed like that, but their future was uncertain—their situation could potentially erupt again at any point but James's gut instinct told him the danger was over, in this lifetime at least.

"Thank you, Cami, I'm sure they'll love it," James said, knowing Cami must have sifted through thousands of photographs and hours of video footage in order to create the album.

"Well, I thought they might as well get something nice out of their experience. I think the best moments are captured when we're not looking at the camera, not trying to smile and appear perfect," Cami said, looking at the gift.

She looked thoughtful, and James wondered if she was thinking of something, or someone, in her own past, but he didn't ask. She never asked about his past, which he appreciated, and in return he never asked about hers. Their pasts were buried in secrecy, and it was best they stayed that way.

Cami looked up again, a faint smile on her lips, a silent understanding. "You should get going," she said, picking up the gift and placing it back in his arms.

The location of the engagement party was a rooftop cocktail bar in Manhattan, the location of Zahra and Jayce's first date. His company was handling security, and upon entering, James immediately located Deacon standing in the corner that gave the best view of the rooftop. James slid between guests and sidled up to his brother.

"How is everything?" James asked, surveying the party.

"Uneventful, as planned. Zahra looks beautiful," Deacon said with a smirk on his face.

James snorted, his gaze landing on her. Her bright green eyes sparkled from where he stood.

"She's taken, Deacon," James said, grinning. Zahra was exactly Deacon's type, but he'd never tell Jayce that, especially after Deacon had kissed her one day in the middle of their case. It had been necessary to test their theory, but Deacon had been a little too quick to put his hand up for the job.

"Things can change," Deacon said, laughing at his own joke.

If there were ever two people truly destined for each other, two people completely in love, it was Zahra and Jayce. James knew Deacon was only joking around—he might want to get into bed with Zahra for a few months, but that's where he would want it to end. Deacon's heart belonged to someone else, someone who had died a terrible death.

Since her death, both James and Deacon had agreed—no girlfriends. They had few rules, but that was one of them and the reason was twofold—the woman would never truly know who she was with, and that didn't make for a great relationship, and purely by association with them, she would have a target hanging over her head.

James and Deacon survived because they knew how to; they had done it all their lives, but it was still a daily fight. A woman could complicate things and create a weak spot in their plans—if you loved someone, you would do anything for them, and your enemies knew that.

"So tell me, how was London?" Deacon asked, looking straight ahead.

"We have a name, but I'm waiting to hear more from Samuel. They are after me, though, not you. The guy said to me 'they have been hunting you.' There was nothing mentioned about you, Deacon. This goes deep into my past, long before we met," James said.

Deacon was silent for a moment. "We'll figure it out," he said confidently.

It wasn't the first time someone had come after James, and it wouldn't be the last. Being a hunted man was a lifelong battle.

James nodded his head, watching Jayce now. And it was almost as if Jayce could feel eyes on him because he lifted his head and cast James a grin.

"I'll be back," James said to Deacon. He walked toward Jayce, who was politely separating himself from the conversation he'd been having. They shook hands in greeting.

"It's good to see you again. How is life in Tokyo?" Jayce asked, patting him on the back.

"Much the same, Jayce, much the same," James said, giving him a teasing smile. Jayce never respected the request not to ask questions about his life, or his past—he just couldn't help himself.

James leaned across, interrupting the conversation quickly, to give Zahra a kiss on the cheek and his congratulations.

"Thank you," Zahra said. "But I'm sure this didn't come as a surprise to you, did it?"

James smiled at Jayce and shrugged his shoulders.

Jayce laughed. "Other than my father, James was the first to know. And he was the first to see the ring. I didn't want to keep it in our apartment until we moved into Luma Street, so I gave it to James to store at Thomas Security. It was probably safer there than it was in the bank vault."

If anyone had asked James if he thought Zahra and Jayce would make it, he would've absolutely said no. But the two of them were a lesson in forgiveness and persistence.

"Can you have a drink tonight?" Jayce asked with mischievous eyes.

"One drink," James said.

Jayce chuckled. "I guess this party is going until noon, then," he said sarcastically, referencing the one and only other time they'd had a drink together.

"Come on." Jayce led him toward an empty couch in the corner and ordered two double whiskeys. "It's technically one drink, Thomas."

James scoffed as he sat on the chair opposite Jayce. "I brought you something," James said, slipping his hand into his inner jacket pocket. He pulled out a small box of Cuban cigars—Kyoji's favorite.

Nostalgia fogged Jayce's eyes and a sad smile formed on his lips. "I've been thinking about him all day," Jayce said, looking at the box.

Kyoji Tohmatsu, Jayce's brother and best friend, had been killed during the case. He'd taken a bullet, one intended for Jayce, and to this date he was the only client ever killed under Thomas Security's watch—that's what could happen when orders are disobeyed. James still had a soft spot for the Tohmatsu brothers, though—they were fiercely loyal, which James respected immensely, and in another life they could've all been friends.

"I thought so, so let's have one for Kyoji," James said, opening the box.

"For Kyoji," Jayce repeated.

James pulled a cutter and a box of matches from his other pocket and they lit up just as the waiter returned with their drinks.

"Can you believe it? We're sitting here at my engagement party?" Jayce asked, shaking his head softly.

James grinned. "I would say stranger things have happened, but I'm not sure they have."

Jayce laughed and winked at him before puffing on the cigar. "So, really, how is life in Tokyo? Any plans to move back to New York?"

James was no longer based in Tokyo, but that was none of Jayce's concern. "We'll see—it always depends on our clients and what they need."

Jayce ran his finger along his jaw, and James knew he was

mentally forming his next question. They always played the same game: Jayce asked questions, James deflected them.

James brought his glass to his lips, but he paused midway, and Jayce didn't miss it. Jayce turned to look over his shoulder as Makaela Ashwood walked directly toward them.

What the hell? James swore silently.

Makaela saw him too and a flash of fear registered in her eyes, and then they darted from side to side like she might run, but she didn't. James noted she drew a deep breath and continued pace beside Zahra.

"There you are," Zahra said, looking at Jayce. "I wanted to finally introduce you to Maya's sister, Mak Ashwood."

Mak Ashwood.

Jayce stood up and extended his hand. Mak shook it and then, following polite protocol, turned to James. "Hello again," she said with a firm, almost questioning, voice.

Jayce's eyes flickered between them and a curious smile teased his lips. "You two know each other?" Jayce asked.

"No, but we were on the same flight today," James answered. "James Thomas," he said, shaking her warm hand. Her skin was soft, but her grip was firm, assertive without being aggressive.

James felt his body react to her touch, and that was a bad sign. Women were a distraction, and right now, more than ever, he needed to be focused.

"You were in Tokyo, Mak?" Jayce asked.

Mak looked confused. "No, I was in London."

Jayce looked at James again, smiling properly now. "What were you doing in London?"

"Working," James said, smiling back at Jayce.

He noticed Mak watching him, looking at him like she didn't trust him.

Jayce rolled his eyes and then turned his attention back to Mak. "So, how is the big case going? I'm looking forward to the trial starting. I've been following it all in the papers."

"Don't you know not to read the papers, Jayce?" Mak asked with a smile.

"This guy," Jayce said, gesturing toward James, "is the owner of Thomas Security, the firm I suggested you get in contact with. You did speak to Maya, right?" Jayce questioned Zahra.

"Yes, she said that she spoke to you," Zahra answered, "but you already had security organized."

James wished he had some clue as to what was going on. He had been overseas for a few months, and Deacon had largely been handling the office and affairs in New York, so he had no idea what case they were talking about.

But if Mak Ashwood's sister was best friends with Zahra, that meant they should have a report on her entire family and Samuel should've sent it through already. *What is taking him so long?*

"That's right. I have a contract in place, and they seem to be doing a good job so I thought additional security was unnecessary," Mak said, looking at James again.

She had a fierceness about her, a resilience in the face of fear. She was brave, James noted.

And she was also tiny with a body that curved in all the right places. The bodice of her gown drew in her waist and pushed up her breasts. Zahra might be Deacon's type, but Mak was definitely his.

"You should change firms," Jayce said matter-of-factly.

Oh, fuck no. That's a very bad idea.

3

MAK ASHWOOD

This can't be happening. Mak cleared her throat.

"I really don't think I need that level of security. Most of the hype around this case is simply that—hype. The security I have is fine." But even as Mak said the words she wondered if they were true. She had reported the scroll incident on her way home from the airport, and her security company was looking into it. She hoped to have more information by morning.

She dared to look at James again, and his eyes were narrowed, like he could read her thoughts.

"Sorry, I got held up back there," Maya said, sashaying in. "Oh, hello, I don't believe we've met," she said, looking at James.

Mak observed her sister as she greeted James, noting that Maya showed none of the fear or distrust Mak felt upon seeing him the first time. *It was all in my head. James runs a security firm. He looks after Jayce and Zahra. He surely had nothing to do with the scroll incident.*

"James Thomas," he said, responding to Maya.

"Oh, you're James Thomas," Maya said. "Mak, this is the man I told you—"

"Yes, yes, I know," Mak said, interrupting her sister. She could not have this conversation again.

"I'm worried she's going to get herself killed," Maya said.

"Maya, this is a conversation we can have another time. It's Zahra and Jayce's engagement party, so let's talk about other things," Mak said, looking at neither her sister nor James. "So, have you set a date yet?"

Zahra smiled, and Maya felt her heart warm at the way Jayce looked at her.

"We have, we set it last night in anticipation for the questions this evening," Zahra said. "July seventeenth, next summer, so keep it free." Zahra nodded her head at all of them in turn, James included.

"And Maya and I are the bridesmaids," Jemma Foster said, slipping in beside her sister. They looked so similar they could be mistaken for twins.

"Mak! How are you doing?" Jemma asked enthusiastically, greeting her with a kiss on the cheek. "I haven't seen you in so long."

"I know, I've been working on the case . . . Not much else to report, unfortunately," Mak said. She could feel James's eyes on her again, and she felt like she was under a microscope. She also felt like he knew she was lying.

A waiter came by with a tray of drinks and Mak grabbed a champagne, as did Jemma.

"Yeah, I've heard about your case. I didn't realize the mob was still such a big deal," Jemma said.

Mak shrugged her shoulders. "They aren't what they used to be in America, but this group has ties to the Camorra—the Italian mafia in the old country. They're a big deal and cover everything from sexual exploitation, firearms trafficking, drugs, counterfeiting, extortion . . . it goes on and on."

Jemma's eyes widened. "So you're going after the big boys? Well, you've got some balls, Mak. You'd better get hot-shot here," she said, nodding to James, "to look after you."

Mak felt her throat constrict.

"Mak can contact us at any time she wants, but it sounds like she's already in good hands," James said.

Mak was grateful, and surprised, that he'd answered for her. She wanted to look at him, to try and read his thoughts, but she knew his face would give away nothing.

"Anyway, let's leave these men alone to smoke their cigars. I just wanted you to finally meet Mak," Zahra said to Jayce. She placed a hand on his chest and a sweet kiss on his lips.

Some days Mak longed for that kind of connection. She was successful, and she loved her career, but she was also lonely at times.

Her skin tingled, and she knew James was watching her again. And she realized what she was doing, as she so often did absentmind-edly—she was twirling her wedding band, which she now wore on her right ring finger.

"Yes, let's go to the bar. I ordered us some special drinks, and they should be ready," Jemma said, wiggling her eyebrows.

"Oh no," Zahra moaned, but Mak was grateful for the escape.

Jemma turned to walk away and Mak smiled at Jayce and James, pulling her eyes away so they didn't linger, and excused herself, following in Maya's footsteps.

They weaved through the other guests until they reach the bar.

"Watermelon mojitos and tequila shots!" Jemma said, smiling proudly as she held out her hands like she was presenting a stage act.

"Oh my, I'm going to feel terrible tomorrow," Maya said, passing around the shots.

"Brunch at Stacie's?" Mak asked, grinning at her sister. Stacie's was a greasy pancake house they frequented when they were hungover. And only when they were hungover.

"Meet you there at eleven," Maya said as she threw back the shot.

The girls followed suit, and Jemma lobbed her hands up in the air. "Let the party begin!"

Mak laughed properly now that she could relax among friends in a high-security environment, and she no longer feared James Thomas attacking her.

"So, Zahra, you didn't tell me your security guy looked like that. Tell me more, please," Maya said.

"I wish I could, but honestly, I barely know anything about him. His name is James Thomas and he owns, and lives at, Thomas Security. And he has a brother, Deacon Thomas, who is standing over there." Zahra looked toward the entrance of the rooftop to a man who flashed a perfect smile back at them as if he knew who they were talking about.

Zahra laughed. "He's probably recording me."

The way she said it sounded like a joke, but there was a seriousness in her eyes.

"Well, if he is, we best put on a good show then. Drink up, ladies," Jemma said.

An hour passed, Mak knew because she'd timed it on her watch, before she allowed herself to look in his direction again. She wanted to watch James, to observe him now that her mind was clear of fear. But when she finally did, the couch had new occupants and James Thomas was nowhere to be seen. She half-listened to the girls chitchat while her eyes roamed over the party, looking for him. She systematically worked her way through the crowd, a decent gathering of guests. She located Jayce, talking with a couple nearby, but James was not with him. Mak's eyes flickered to James's brother, who was in position by the entrance now, but he was talking on his phone, his eyes looking straight ahead as he spoke.

Had James left already? Her eyes did one more sweep. He was definitely no longer at the party but he was still in her thoughts. What was it about him that was so mysterious? So alluring?

It was three in the morning before they left the party, escorted out by Thomas Security. Mak's car was waiting for her when she stepped onto the sidewalk. The wind had picked up during the evening and a gust blew her gown so that it billowed behind her. Mak said her goodbyes, promising to meet Maya for brunch, and then climbed into the backseat of the car. Her bodyguard closed the door then sat in the front seat, next to the driver.

She rubbed her eyes as she struggled to see straight. She'd had way too much to drink—they all had, courtesy of Jemma Foster's encouragement—and she knew she would pay for it tomorrow. But tonight, right now, she didn't care. It numbed her anxiety—the anxiety of finding the scroll, the anxiety of taking on a high-profile case she could lose in humiliating style, and the anxiety of meeting James Thomas, who had vanished like a ghost and had not reappeared all night.

"Is there an update on the scroll I received at the hotel?" Mak asked the men in the front seats.

"No," said her bodyguard. "At this stage we don't have any leads. It looks like the hotel's security tapes have been tampered with. We'll continue looking at it, and I'll provide you with another update in the morning."

Mak chewed on her lip—that wasn't the response she wanted. "Okay," she said with a flat voice. What else could she say?

She rested her head against the window, the alcohol and jetlag catching up with her. The motion of the car lured her to a light sleep, her mind only vaguely aware of the series of turns the vehicle made. What felt like seconds later, she was being woken up: she was home.

Her bodyguard opened the door and walked her up the steps of her Upper East Side apartment building. She was accompanied in, and once her apartment was checked, she closed the door behind her bodyguard and sighed in relief. She leaned one palm against the door while she kicked off her shoes, leaving them where they landed, and stumbled into the bathroom. She made a futile attempt to remove her makeup and brush her teeth. She was drunk and dead tired and wanted nothing more than to curl up in bed. Mak unzipped her gown and let it fall to the floor, and then pushed aside the bed cushions enough to climb onto her side of the bed. Even though her husband had never returned home, she still slept on the same side, still thought of it as her side of the bed.

Mak was peeling back the duvet when she saw it. She blinked twice, not trusting her drunken mind and eyes, but she hadn't made a mistake. Her pulse erupted like fireworks on the Fourth of July as she picked up another scroll, hidden behind the cushions. She ripped off the ribbon and unrolled it.

Keep your eyes open, Makaela.

Mak's hand went to her throat. Fear latched itself on like the tentacles of an octopus, strangling her as she struggled to breathe.

They are doing this to scare you, she told herself. *Calm down. Don't let them win.*

4

JAMES THOMAS

The street was quiet, the moon casting a soft glow over the night. Most people were afraid of the dark, but James loved the dark—he felt safer in the dark, he always had. He sat silently in his car, looking at the ninth floor. One light was on in Mak Ashwood's apartment. It had been on all night, and it was nearing sunrise. He had to assume she'd fallen asleep with the light on—she'd certainly been drunk enough.

Samuel had finally called in with the report, and now James knew why it had taken so long. The phone call had come not long after the girls had excused themselves to the bar, and now he wished he'd never asked Samuel for the report. He wished he didn't know what he did. Her husband wasn't only missing, he had put money in several offshore bank accounts. A lot of money. Mak Ashwood was six million dollars richer than she thought.

What had her husband been up to? How did a twenty-two-year-old accumulate that kind of money? Six one-million-dollar deposits made annually that hadn't been touched. Not a single withdrawal had been made from any of the accounts.

James had left the party early, but he'd only gone as far as his car parked on the street where he sat and read the report over and over again.

Why was Mak Ashwood on his flight? Why could he not ignore his attraction to her? Why did he ask Samuel for the report? His own behavior was so out of character, and that filled him with apprehension.

What he was doing now, though, he knew the answer to. After he read the report he'd decided to test her security. She was using a decent firm, but he wanted to make sure they were doing their job because for all he knew, the guys she was prosecuting might not be her biggest concern.

James had followed her car to her apartment, and they had failed to see they had a tail. And he parked straight outside her apartment; they had failed to notice that as well. That meant she had the minimum possible security on her, and they weren't surveying her environment. Or they were doing a really shitty job. He wanted to ask Samuel to tap her phone and monitor the communication with her security company, but he drew the line there. This had gone too far already, and if he asked Samuel to do that, Samuel would mention it to Deacon. And that was a conversation James didn't want to have.

James sighed, leaning his head against the headrest.

Interestingly, Mak Ashwood had never sought to have her husband declared deceased, so she was still legally a married woman. James had seen enough missing persons cases to know that when a spouse goes missing, the other usually seeks a court order to have them declared deceased so they could have some form of closure and move on with their lives. Sometimes it happened after a few years, sometimes five years, most of the time at ten years. And almost definitely after thirteen years. So why hadn't Mak done the same thing? Could she really believe he might come home one day?

Mak had been married for less than a year when her husband disappeared, and she was only thirty-five now. She could still meet someone, still have a family, but she hadn't moved on from him. The report detailed the private investigator she'd hired to look for him, and James wondered how he'd failed to find the offshore accounts. *If she'd hired me, I would've found him. Or his body.*

Pink streaks ribboned through the sky as the sun began to rise, and James turned the key in the ignition. It was time to go home, time to sleep. James drove through the deserted streets, downtown to Thomas Security.

She's not my problem. He wished he'd never met her, and he wished she'd never penetrated his mind. In only a few hours she'd consumed his thoughts—thoughts that should be focused solely on his own survival. He had his own security situation to deal with, and it was a much more perilous situation than hers. Someone had found him again and they were going to come for him—if he didn't find them first.

The walls of Samuel's office looked like a pinboard of screens, all locked together, capable of projecting one big image or multiple smaller images. Every time Samuel put in a request for a new piece of equipment, James approved it without asking a single question— Samuel always got what he wanted because he never let James down.

Samuel pushed his glasses up the ridge of his nose with his index finger. "Do any of these men look familiar?" he asked.

The wall of televisions transformed to show a series of surveillance images. James studied them, one by one, as he knew Deacon was doing beside him.

James sighed. "No." He turned his head to his brother, who shook his head without taking his eyes off the screen.

"These are known associates of Escanta. It's an organization shrouded in secrecy, and I'm finding it difficult to determine its origins, or its time of inception. I believe, at this stage, that its roots are Russian."

James had expected as much—he and the Russians had a damaged relationship.

"Escanta isn't a Russian name, is it?" Deacon asked, his eyebrows pinching together.

"No, and I think that's deliberate. This group is very private, and very elite, but I'm not sure we should mistake that for small—it might be a branch of a larger group."

"What does Escanta specialize in?" James asked.

Samuel clasped his fingers together. "That's the kicker," he said. "I don't know."

"But they have to make money somehow," James said.

"Sure they do, and I'm working on it. Time, James, I need more time," Samuel said, casting him a look like a father might give his impatient son.

James blew out a frustrated breath. "I need to be on the ground. I need to go to Russia—"

"You're not going anywhere," Deacon said, quick to shut down the idea. "Give Samuel more time. We're safe for the moment."

"I don't think this involves you, Deacon," James said, and Samuel looked like he agreed.

"Perhaps not directly, but we're in this together. If they're hunting you, they might as well be hunting me."

Samuel's lips turned up in a proud smile. They didn't have family, but they had each other.

James's phone vibrated, and he looked at the caller ID: *Jayce Tohmatsu*.

"Jayce," James said, surprised to hear from him. Calls from his number were, thankfully, rare lately.

"James. What are you doing?"

James laughed. "Working. What do you want?"

"A favor," Jayce said.

"A favor?" James asked, eyeballing Deacon.

Deacon made a twirling motion with his index finger and Samuel converted the call to play through the speaker.

"Go ahead," James said curiously.

"Mak Ashwood. I received a call from her today asking if I could put her in touch with Thomas Security."

James cringed internally. It had been three days since he'd seen Mak Ashwood, and he was doing everything possible to keep her out of his mind. But here she was again, back in his world—in the worst possible way.

"Why the change? She seemed confident in her security at your party," James said.

"I don't know, I didn't ask the question. Can you meet with her?"

James looked to Deacon, who seemed nonchalant about the idea. James knew it was a bad idea to take her on as a client—he was already more involved than he should've been. James didn't need to look at Samuel to know what he was thinking.

James stalled. "A favor? What might you do to return the favor, if I should ever need it?"

Jayce scoffed and then paused, as if he were thinking it through. "Maybe I'll build you the next Thomas Security headquarters, you know, when you outgrow that one."

James grinned. Jayce would love that because he'd know every intricate detail of their building and Jayce loved to know the inside facts. "I see. We're not taking on any new clients, Jayce, you know that. We took on your family to repay a favor from Kyoji—it was an exception."

The conversation had Deacon's attention now because he knew James was stalling.

"I know, but I'm asking you to make a concession and meet with her at least—her family is apparently very worried about her."

"We'll meet with her, Jayce, but I'm not making any promises."

An annoyed groan came through the line. "Fine. Today? What time should I tell her?"

James rolled his eyes again, and Deacon chuckled. Jayce personified efficiency. "We'll see her today and we'll call her with the details and arrange a car for her."

"Thanks, I appreciate it," Jayce said before hanging up.

James put his phone down on the table.

Deacon raised one eyebrow. "What was that about?"

James cleared his throat and crossed his leg over his knee. He had to be honest, as much as he wanted to hide the truth. "She's a distraction."

He'd expected Deacon to be concerned but instead he did something completely unexpected: he laughed.

"You think this is funny?" James asked.

"I'm sorry, I . . . I've never heard those words from your mouth," Deacon said, fighting to control himself.

She's a distraction. It was their code when women were involved. Deacon had used it several times in the past, but it was the first time James had used it. He normally prided himself on his ability to block out desirable women, but Mak Ashwood had undone him.

"So what do you want to do?" Deacon asked.

James rubbed his eyes. "We'll meet with her and see what's going on. If we take her on, though, I'm not working with her. You're going to have to be the main contact."

Deacon's face beamed a pretty-boy smile. "Okay, let's see what the *five-foot beauty* who has James all flustered has to say."

Deacon and Samuel smiled at each other and James was just grateful Samuel had kept his mouth shut thus far.

The blows came at him, hard and fast.

"Again," James said, not giving his sparring partner a chance to rest.

An expletive fell from his partner's mouth but the man straightened up and focused.

"Your left is still too weak," James said. "You need to work on it."

He was in a training session, passing time until Mak arrived. They had personal trainers who worked with their bodyguards, but every few months James and Deacon tested them themselves. They expected them to be the best—nothing less was acceptable when someone's life was in their hands.

"Again," James said.

His partner looked like he might fall over at any minute, or vomit, but James pushed him harder. After another two rounds, he called time.

"Well done," James said, patting him on the back. "I have a meeting soon, but I'll make some notes and have them sent to you. Discuss them with your trainer and make sure that left arm is a priority."

It was natural for righties to be weak in the left hand, but if you worked for Thomas Security, you'd better be able to throw a punch with your left just as hard as your right.

His partner didn't speak as he grappled for air, simply nodding his head instead. James grabbed his towel and phone and headed to his apartment. He showered, changed into a clean sweater and jeans, his daily uniform, and was back downstairs with five minutes to spare. He found Deacon in Samuel's office.

"Ready?" Deacon asked with a lopsided smile.

"Yes, Deacon," James said, leading the way downstairs to the boardroom. Samuel wouldn't join them but he'd be witness to every-thing that went on via a surveillance system. Every single room in Thomas Security had full surveillance, including their apartments.

James pushed the sleeves of his sweater up as he sat down. He felt warm, a result of the training session and the anticipation churning inside him.

The phone rang and Deacon answered it. "Send her up," he said.

She's here. He didn't want to see her; he wanted to forget her. But he did want to know why she was here. Why had she changed her mind? What had happened in the last seventy-two hours?

"Take charge of this meeting, Deacon," James said. "I want to be involved as little as possible."

Deacon nodded his head, his assessing gaze unnerving James. Deacon still didn't know James had already pulled reports on Mak, otherwise he would've surely said something, and he definitely didn't know he'd followed her car home.

The door opened and James assumed his role, showing no emotion whatsoever.

"Mak, I'm Deacon Thomas," Deacon said, moving forward to

shake her hand. "You've already met James." He closed the door behind her.

James moved forward to shake her hand and when he touched her he felt it again—the tightening of his chest and his already warm body heating further.

"Mak," James said, nodding his head. He sat down beside his brother, and Mak sat opposite them.

"So, how can we help you?" Deacon asked and in return Mak looked at him when she spoke—exactly as James had intended.

"Thank you for meeting me today," she said, her voice calm but strong. "I have a situation," she continued, "and you come highly recommended, obviously."

"We know about the case you're working on, but we were surprised to receive your call. Our understanding is that you already have security in place," Deacon said.

"I do have security in place, but I'm not sure they are sufficient for the job. I asked them to look into a few things, and they haven't been able to give me the answers I need. Jayce Tohmatsu seems to think you can find out anything, hence why I'm here."

James was intrigued.

"What has changed, Mak?" Deacon asked.

Mak rubbed her lips together and James's eyes lingered on them, wondering what they would taste like. He noticed Mak hadn't looked at him yet. Was she avoiding his gaze?

"There have been two separate security breaches. One in my hotel room in London, and one in my apartment. My security firm can't provide any information on either, other than advising me that the hotel's security tapes have been tampered with."

"We need details, Mak, to understand the situation. Anything you say is completely confidential, whether we have a security contract with you or not," Deacon said.

Her chest rose as she inhaled. "Two notes, on delicate paper rolled up like a scroll and tied with a red ribbon. The first one said: 'Death is but an illusion, as you will soon see.' The second one said: 'Keep your eyes open, Makaela.'"

Fuck, this is bad.

James looked at Deacon, who looked genuinely surprised.

"Where are you staying now?" Deacon asked.

Mak's eyes flickered between Deacon and James. "In my apartment."

Deacon shook his head. "They got into your apartment once, and if they want to, they will do it again. You should not be staying there, I can tell you that already. We'll book you into a secure hotel until suitable accommodation can be arranged."

"Who do you think is doing this?" James asked, speaking for the first time.

Mak met his gaze, unwavering. "It would have to be related to the case I'm working on. I think they're trying to scare me, to intimidate me. They're the mob—they think laws don't apply to them, that their crimes should go unpunished. And the fact that a female, younger than the average prosecutor, took on this case . . . Well, I don't think they like it very much."

It wasn't what she said, but the way she said it. It wasn't just her looks he was attracted to, it was her demeanor and her courage. She was too tempting, too much of a distraction. James knew in that instant they couldn't take the case.

James took control of the meeting. "The level of security you have on you is completely inadequate and Deacon is right, you can't stay at your apartment. The security plan we would create for you would be detailed, and resource intensive, which we currently don't have. It's a much more complicated case then we'd initially assumed, and I don't think we're the right firm for you at this moment. What we'll do is arrange your security for the next forty-eight hours while we source an alternative firm and consult with them to create a plan."

Deacon looked at James calmly, but James knew he no longer thought the distraction was funny.

"He's right, Mak. And we'll cover you so you're safe until everything is sorted," Deacon finally said.

Mak's eyes stayed on James, and he felt like he was going to start sweating.

"You looked after the entire Tohmatsu family, including Zahra Foster. I am one person, and you don't have the resources to cover me?"

"We took on two big clients last week; it's just bad timing," James said, his face as impassive as hers.

"But you don't take on new clients," she argued back.

"Ordinarily, no, we don't. But as we had the resources available, primarily those no longer allocated to the Tohmatsu family, when we were approached, we took the offer."

"Why did you meet me if you can't take on any new clients?"

"As I said, your case is more complex than we first realized. We would put you under twenty-four-hour surveillance, a personal bodyguard, bodyguards surveying your environment twenty-four hours a day, upgrade the security at your office, provide you with a personal driver, change your apartment, etc. We're good at what we do because we don't take any risks with our clients. It's extreme, or it's nothing. We don't do in-between, because that's when people get hurt. We will find you a good firm that has the resources to put our plan in place."

She raised her eyebrows, transferring her penetrating gaze to Deacon.

"Jayce said he wouldn't use anyone else, that Thomas Security is the best. So who are you going to recommend?" Mak questioned.

Deacon spoke up. "Truthfully, I don't know yet. We've collaborated with other firms in the past, so it will be one of those, but we need to speak to them first and assess the situation. That's why we said we'll cover you for the next forty-eight hours, until we can get this sorted. You don't need to do anything. Go back to your office, in one of our cars. We'll send a bodyguard with you, and we'll organize your accommodation for this evening. Tomorrow, we'll get back to you with an update. Let us handle this, please. You need security, and you need it now."

She pressed her lips together again and then said, "Okay. Thank you."

"Right, give us five minutes to get a bodyguard and a car organized, and we'll get you back to your office. We'll make sure you're taken care of, I promise," Deacon said.

James and Deacon stood up and walked silently to Samuel's office, but James knew the wrath that was coming. They never argued in front of anyone but Samuel and Cami, because they were family.

When the door closed, it started.

"Really? This situation isn't funny anymore. You can't trust yourself to stay out of it, even with me managing her case? What exactly is going on here?" Deacon made no effort to conceal his displeasure at the situation.

"I'm doing everyone a favor. And if her case gets as complicated as I think it's going to, we're going to have to work on it together." James didn't completely answer Deacon's question, but he had a valid point, and his brother knew it.

Deacon's jaw sawed back and forth and then he turned to Samuel, who was watching quietly from behind his desk. "Run a security report on Mak Ashwood and find out which of our hotels have availability."

Samuel faltered for a fraction of a second and anyone would've missed it, but not Deacon. And not James.

"What?" Deacon asked.

James didn't want to put Samuel in the middle of this. "He already has the reports. I asked him to run them. Mak Ashwood was on my flight from London. The engagement party wasn't the first time I saw her, but it was the first time I met her, properly at least."

Deacon's eyes blazed. "You should've fucking told me before that meeting. You should've said no to Jayce, and you should never have put yourself in this situation. Why are you doing this? Is it because of what happened in Paris?"

"It's got nothing to do with that," James said, although he wasn't entirely convinced of that himself.

Deacon eyeballed him, no doubt trying to work out if he was lying or not.

"If it's got nothing to do with that, then I don't fucking understand this at all. This is so unlike you," Deacon said.

"I'm doing the right thing by not taking her on as a client," James repeated, refusing to raise his voice in retaliation.

"You did the right thing in the meeting, but every other move you've made has been wrong. Why didn't you tell me?"

"Because I assumed you would react exactly as you are," James said.

"No, I'm reacting like this because you're being secretive with Samuel, and I'm not entirely sure you're being honest about the level of your feelings for her, either. I don't know what you were even thinking by meeting with her."

Deacon's fury was rising and James didn't have an answer—he wasn't sure what he felt or why he had done it either. James did know, however, it wasn't just this situation that had triggered his brother's emotions.

When James didn't respond—refusing to engage in a yelling match—it only infuriated his brother further.

Deacon glared at him. "How do you think that we, that you, are any different from the men she talked about in the meeting? She's a criminal prosecutor! She abides by the law. She loathes men like you."

"Don't make this personal, Deacon," James said. He knew that underneath the words Deacon was trying to protect him, to deter him from pursuing her, but his words still hurt—because they were true.

"This," Deacon said, "is a fucking disaster waiting to happen. I'm sorting her out. You stay here, and you stay out of this!" Deacon slammed the door behind him and James tilted his head back and looked at the ceiling.

"He's overreacting, but you understand why, right?" Samuel said quietly.

"Yeah," James said. "He's thinking about Nicole."

5

MAK ASHWOOD

The silence was corrupted with awkwardness, and no one but Mak seemed to notice.

"You're very quiet," Mak said to her temporary bodyguard, Cami.

Cami gave her a smile that reached her eyes. "I can be talkative too. It all depends on you. Some clients love to chatter away, others like to pretend we don't exist. I don't mind either way, but I usually leave it up to the client to choose whether to engage or not."

Mak nodded her head. "I see. How long have you worked at Thomas Security?"

"From the beginning—I was one of their first employees," she said without elaborating.

"How many female bodyguards do they have?" Mak said, the question two-fold. She was curious to know how many females worked in the private security industry, Mak assumed a low percentage, and she was also slyly trying to gain more information about Cami's rank—she wanted to know if Deacon Thomas gave her one of his best bodyguards.

Cami sighed, shaking her head. "Not enough. I think there are . . . nine of us. It's very much a male-dominated field but that gives us women an advantage: we're always underestimated. In fact, I nearly kicked Deacon's ass yesterday. Nearly, but not quite. I'll get there, though," she said with a laugh.

"Deacon's ass, huh? And what about James's ass?"

Cami chuckled softly. "No, there's no beating James. Deacon has, but only once, and James was sick with a cold. We all have our different strengths, though. If we got into a car chase, you would want Deacon driving, not James." Cami looked directly at Mak, her eyes soft and comforting. "You're going to be okay, Mak. You'll be well protected, even if it's not with Thomas Security."

Mak nodded her head but her emotions were still thrown from that meeting. She'd thought Deacon was the one calling the shots but ultimately it had been James's decision. It seemed a legitimate excuse not to take her on, and she wouldn't want someone doing a sub-par job, but there was something hiding behind those black eyes.

"Jayce said Thomas Security is the best, and he wouldn't work with anyone else," Mak said, testing Cami now.

Her head rocked from side to side. "It depends on the case and what the client needs. I haven't seen your full case details, so I can't comment, but I know with certainty the brothers won't pass your case on to someone they don't trust."

It was a roundabout, dodging kind of answer. Mak focused her questioning back on Cami. "So, if you nearly beat Deacon, you must be good, then."

Cami scoffed. "Of course I am, and I've worked for it. You know, you and I are more alike than you probably realize. I've followed your case in the papers, for the same reason I think it's intrigued a lot of people. It isn't just about the case, it's about you. A young, female lawyer taking on big cases with big risks. I hate to say it, but it's some-thing still out of the ordinary. It's quite courageous, really. And I've had to do the same thing, albeit in a different industry. I trained with the best, and I stepped up for the cases others didn't want to take. I pushed forward, so to speak, and I didn't take no for an answer."

"What did you do before working for Thomas Security?" Mak asked.

"I worked," Cami said, her eyes sparkling with secrets.

Mak smiled. "I see. So, what happens from here?"

Cami shifted, crossing her legs toward Mak. "I will shadow you for the next forty-eight hours. I'll be in the office with you, escort you back to the hotel, stay in the suite next to you, and then repeat it all. Once Deacon has organized the logistics of your security and completed the handover, I'll be relieved by your permanent bodyguard."

"Right. Will my new bodyguard also be female?"

"Not necessarily. Sometimes we will try and put a female bodyguard on a client, particularly when we don't want the bodyguard to look like security as such. Again it depends on the case. I wasn't chosen today because I'm female, though; they just want to make sure you're safe, and I'm damn good at my job."

Mak laughed—she already liked this girl. It was a shame it was going to be a short-lived relationship.

When they arrived at the office, Mak was quickly escorted inside by Cami, who then did a surveillance check of her office while Mak sat down at her desk and lost herself in files of evidence and notes relating to her case. She had one week until her next court date, and there was never such a thing as being over-prepared. She made a checklist of items to be covered in her meeting tomorrow with the homicide detectives and another checklist of witness preparations. When Mak looked up from her files, she realized it was nearly ten o'clock and neither of them had eaten. Was she supposed to organize food for Cami? She didn't know the protocols.

"Cami?" Mak asked. "Are you hungry? I'm going to order in some food."

"Sure. I'll eat anything, so you tell me what you want and I'll organize it."

Mak raised her eyebrows in surprise. "Um, okay, let's order something relatively healthy, seeing as I'm probably not going to get to a barre class this week. How about a chicken salad?"

"Sure, consider it done," Cami said.

While Cami stepped out of Mak's office, presumably to order the food, Mak did what she'd been longing to do all night, and what she should've done on the weekend had she not been so distracted by the second scroll.

After receiving the note, she'd stayed awake all night—the fear obliterating her tiredness. She'd taken a knife from the kitchen block, however useless the idea, and inspected every inch of her apartment. She'd then barricaded the front door, sliding a dining chair under the handle, and huddled on the sofa until sunrise. When her security guys arrived they took the scroll, installed additional cameras in her apartment, and told her not to leave without a bodyguard. But Deacon Thomas was right: if they'd gotten in before, they would get in again. And next time they might leave more than just a scroll behind for her.

Mak opened up Google and typed *James Thomas* into the search bar.

It was a common name and millions of results came up but nothing seemingly relevant.

Thomas Security

No website, no phone number, nothing. Mak hit the *News* tab but it proved fruitless.

Maybe I'm going about this the wrong way. This time she typed *Jayce Tohmatsu*. If you want to find the security, find the client. Hundreds of news items surfaced but Mak didn't have time to look through them as Cami walked back in, closing the door behind her. Mak quickly closed the browser and reopened her email. Although Cami probably couldn't see her screen, it wasn't a risk Mak wanted to take.

Forget him. You shouldn't even be looking him up. The voice in her head was the sensible voice, the one that obeyed logic and reason. But still she wanted to know. She couldn't forget his eyes, the way he looked at her, the way his hand had felt wrapped around hers. He was like a puzzle waiting to be solved.

Her office phone rang and she jumped, piquing Cami's attention.

Mak took a settling breath before she answered.

"Mak Ashwood."

"Mak. Hi, it's Jared from forensics. You're there late."

"I'm one week out, so I'm going to be here late every night," Mak said. "What's up?"

"I ran the DNA analysis from those two unsolved murder cases you asked me about. Unfortunately there wasn't a match, not even close."

Hmm. She was sure there was a link in the cases, but she couldn't find it. She made a note to review the evidence again. "Thanks anyway, Jared."

"You're welcome. So, in this crazy schedule of yours, do you have time for a drink?"

Mak should've been expecting this. They'd been flirting for months, but, with the case building, she hadn't given him much thought these past few weeks.

"Um, things are . . ." She looked across to Cami, who seemed to be paying her no attention, but she thought that unlikely. "Can I get back to you tomorrow evening? I've just got to sort a few things out, and then I'll know where I'm at."

There was a brief silence on the line before he answered. "Sure, just let me know. I'll leave you to it."

He didn't sound pissed off, but he didn't sound thrilled either. If he'd asked a week ago, she would've said yes, but so much had changed in a week.

"The food is here," Cami said, standing up.

Mak nodded her head and wrote down Jared's name on her to-do list. She should meet up with him, after all she had no reason not to. She'd call him back tomorrow and agree to a drink. God knew she could use one to relax after the past few days. She felt wound up like a jack-in-the-box ready to spring out, scaring the living hell out of whoever was around.

While Cami was out of the room, she reopened the browser, and at the same time her mind repeated the words: *Forget him.*

She did it anyway, quickly browsing through the articles. She doubted he would be mentioned in any of the speculative pieces on

Jayce's family so she kept scrolling until she came across the articles from Kyoji's funeral. There it was: a picture of Jayce, Zahra, and James. Given the angle of the photo, the camera was taken from the right side of the path that led to the temple. Jayce's and Zahra's bodies were obscured by another body—one dressed in a suit with his hand over his face. Despite not being able to view him properly, she knew it was James Thomas. He made it look incidental, but Mak thought it was a completely intentional move—it was like he knew where the camera was, and he didn't want to have his photo taken.

So, Zahra and Jayce knew nothing about him, and the Internet— the holy Mecca of information—knew nothing about him, either.

Who are you, James Thomas?

6

JAMES THOMAS

James took the stairs two at a time until he reached the rooftop. The bulletproof glass dome above the Thomas Security headquarters was the safest place to get a sense of being outside, without actually being outside. It had been a luxury to build it, but they spent more time up there than anywhere else.

James spotted Deacon lying on the lounge chair, gazing up at the stars. It had been two days since they'd spoken—the longest James could ever remember.

He walked forward and sat on the spare lounge chair, resting his elbows on his knees.

"I'm sorry; I should've told you," James said. *No secrets* was one of the few other rules they had.

Deacon sighed and sat up to face James.

"Just so you realize, *she's a distraction* is code for I want to get in bed and fuck this girl's brains out for three months. And even *that* we know is a bad idea. It isn't code for I can't stop thinking about this girl," Deacon said.

"I know," James said, frowning.

"I'm sorry about what I said . . . You're not a bad person, James," Deacon said.

"No, you're right—that is who I am. I can justify it all I want: the military or the agency ordered it, I was being hunted, whatever. At the end of the day I've killed hundreds of people and the reality is that I don't feel any remorse. I am the kind of man she hates."

"You're not. We might be the kind of guys who think our crimes should go unpunished, and that the laws don't apply to us—Samuel in particular," Deacon said, smirking, "but we don't do these things out of greed. The men we hurt deserve it. I like to think of us as a balancing force in this world. If I didn't, I'd probably hate myself so much I'd take my own life."

It was the difference between them. Deacon reflected on life, analyzed the things he'd done, questioned the orders and motives of the military. James didn't—he didn't look back at all. What was the point?

"Are you sure this doesn't have anything to do with Paris?" Deacon asked. "You say you're fine, and you act like nothing has changed, but it has. And no one can possibly go through something so traumatic without it having an impact of some kind. You can talk to me about this, James. You don't have to deal with it on your own."

"I know that I can, but there's simply no point in reliving it over and over again. I made a mistake, a grave one, and I have to live with that, but it doesn't mean I should wallow in my grief every day," James said.

"I'm not saying you should, but something like that takes time to get over, and you're not giving yourself any time," Deacon said, searching James's eyes.

Deacon shook his head. "Nicole's death was years ago, and I still remember it so vividly." Deacon scrunched up his face as the vision pained him. "I see five men raping her until she's a bloody mess, and then mutilate her until she passes out from the pain. I see it all, and worst of all I remember lying there, incapacitated. They made me watch when they knew I couldn't do anything. I see her eyes pleading with me, begging me to help her, and I couldn't."

James knew Deacon still relived the horror of Nicole's death because every now and then his screams penetrated the walls of their apartments in the dark hours of the night. James doubted Deacon would ever fully heal, not when he held on to so much regret.

"It wasn't worth it, James. I think of the beautiful moments we shared, the love we shared . . ." He shook his head. "It wasn't worth it. If someone had told me how it would end, I would never have gotten involved. I would've walked away, no matter how hard it would've been." Deacon looked up at the stars.

"I still think about it too, Deacon. If I could've gotten there earlier, I could've stopped it all," James said.

"I don't know how you managed to find us at all, let alone get there earlier. Some days I wished you'd gotten there later, after they'd killed me. It's not right that she was tortured and died because of me, and yet I'm still alive." Deacon sighed. "If they did that to Nicole, what do you think they would do to your girlfriend? I mean, my past is bad, but yours is worse—much worse. You make me look like a fucking apprentice. It's not worth the risk, James. I'm begging you, stay away from this girl. She doesn't deserve it. And neither do you."

"I know she doesn't," James said quietly, for once wishing his life was different, wishing he could have a normal relationship, wishing he could have a life where he didn't need to look over his shoulder at every shadow that passed behind him. That was the change in him since Paris—it had made him consider things, wish for things, that he never had in the past.

"I followed her home, too, from the engagement party," James said, confessing all of his sins.

"Fucking hell," Deacon said, shaking his head.

"I just wanted to test her security. I drove close enough that they should've picked up a tail and they didn't. And I parked right outside her apartment, and they didn't notice that either."

Deacon pulled his lips to one side, mulling it over. "Well, she's changing firms, so I suppose it doesn't matter. Did Samuel know this, too? I don't like the two of you keeping secrets from me."

"I didn't tell Samuel. But you know what he's like . . ." James said with a hint of a smile. "I think he's always spying on us, always keeping tabs. I'm sure he knew I was there, but he hasn't mentioned it to me."

Deacon nodded his head, seeming to agree. "If you were to live your life over, would you make the same choices?" he asked.

"I don't know, Deacon. I don't regret choosing to join the Army—God only knows where I would've ended up without that structure and guidance. But crossing over into the CIA—that wasn't a good choice. But I'm the perfect recruit, right? An orphan with a Delta Force skill set and no family to leave behind. They made such an enticing offer, but I had no idea what I was getting into and what the long-term consequences would be. And Paris . . . Well, I definitely wouldn't make the same choices there, but regardless, it's well and truly done now."

"I wouldn't do it again," Deacon said. "I would choose another life."

His regret hung in the air like thick smog.

"Don't tell me anything about Mak, Deacon. I don't want to know. But make sure she's okay, keep an eye on them."

Deacon nodded his head and James trusted him. He and Samuel would watch over her security, by whatever means necessary. It was the last he would see of Mak Ashwood because Deacon was right, she didn't deserve a death like Nicole's—and that was, without a doubt, what would happen if she were his girlfriend, and he couldn't protect her.

James heard the rooftop door open and close.

"Are we all friends again?" Cami said from behind James. She patted him on the shoulder as she sat down beside him.

Deacon scoffed. "We're always friends."

"Good to hear," Cami said, sipping on a bottle of water.

Cami had been absent for the past few days and James didn't need to ask to know where she'd been. Deacon would've assigned her to Mak, and the fact that she was back indicated Mak's security had been transferred.

"How are you?" Deacon asked, taking the bottle of water from her hands and guzzling the rest of it.

Cami narrowed her eyes at him but didn't reprimand him. "Good. All is good."

All is good was code for *Mak is good.*

"Any updates from Samuel?" Cami asked James.

"No, and he's been working so hard he's barely slept in days," James said. "I need to get on the ground. I need to go to Russia."

Having a guy like Samuel on your team was like having a secret weapon, but every now and then you had to do it old-school style— you had to get on your own two feet and chase down the leads. However, Russia presented a problem. Deacon would want to come with him, but James wanted Deacon in New York to make sure Mak's new security firm was performing.

"I'll go with you," Cami said. "Someone has to stay here and run Thomas Security, and I sure as fuck don't want to do that, so I'll go with you, and Deacon can manage everything here."

"I don't like this," Deacon said immediately.

"I like it a lot," James said, grinning at Cami. She'd been with him on several missions, he'd even taken her into the lair to clean up the mess Kyoji Tohmatsu had made, and she'd performed every time. She was the next best thing to Deacon, and she was the solution to his problem.

"It's sorted, then," she said confidently. "When do you want to leave?"

Deacon groaned but didn't object. He knew James was right about being on the ground—they'd given Samuel more time, but he was running up against a wall every time. They'd find new leads in Russia, give the information to Samuel, and then go from there.

"The day after tomorrow," James said.

It was easier to forget the sense of loneliness he'd felt since Paris during the daylight hours. James worked out, trained his staff, and ran his business. But the dark hours passed as slowly as a leaking tap filled a swimming pool. And his thoughts kept going back to Mak

Ashwood. He had been instantly attracted to her, and that attraction had not dissipated in the days since he'd seen her last. Why? He'd been able to forget other beautiful women in his past, but he was having trouble getting Mak out of his mind. A relationship could never be anything more than a dream—not for him, not given his past. James would put a target on her head, and if things took a turn for the worst, what would he do? James could disappear overnight, but what about her? She had a big family and a great career, and all of that would be gone. She'd have nothing but him and, even if he could protect her, she'd eventually resent him for ruining her life. And that was provided she could even love the man he was. It was impossible—every way he looked at it, it wasn't meant to be.

"Can I offer you something to read during the flight?"

James smiled at the flight attendant but shook his head.

"Yes, please," Cami said from the chair beside him and took two newspapers.

James closed his eyes again. He wondered what Mak thought about the situation she was in, about Thomas Security not taking her on as a client. Was she angry? Was she worried about her new contract? He wanted to know the answers, and he didn't—he wanted to forget her. He needed to forget her.

"You can read this—she's not in it," Cami said, placing a paper on his lap.

It was the first time Cami had mentioned her. James opened his eyes. "I'm not interested in reading it. The news I'm interested in hasn't made the headlines yet," James said.

"Suit yourself," Cami said quietly as she opened the second newspaper.

A thought occurred to James. "Did Deacon instruct you to do that?"

She put the paper down. "No, James, he didn't. I genuinely want to read the paper, seeing as we have nothing else to do on this flight and you're hardly in a talkative mood. But if Deacon had, would you blame him?"

"So you've all had a meeting about this, then?"

Cami sighed. "No, we had a meeting to discuss Mak's strategy and prepare a handover for the firm taking her on. To be honest, I think it's sad."

"Sad?" James repeated.

"I want you to be happy, James. You've been alone most of your life and it would be nice for you to share it with someone, to open up to someone—especially now. But the reality is it's just not in our cards. I don't know . . . I think if you really want a girlfriend, you have to at least choose someone who understands our life, and someone who has our kind of training and can protect themselves," Cami said.

"Yeah, why don't I find another woman from the CIA so she can inform on me again," James said, his voice sounding pained even to his own ears.

He didn't have to pretend with Cami—she was one of the few people he could let his guard down with. Cami had become like a younger sister to him, someone he protected fiercely, but she was also someone who could look after herself.

"Do you remember what you said to me when I made the choice to go deep into the agency?" Her brown eyes were soft and gentle, but she didn't wait for him to respond, because she knew he didn't want to be reminded. "You said to me: love them enough to let them go. Love my family enough to protect them, to let them think I was dead."

"I don't love this girl, Cami," James said. "I barely know her."

"I know that, but it's not the point I'm trying to make. If you want to do what's best for her, that's for her to forget you exist, and you know it. That girl's got enough on her plate without the turmoil you'll bring. I love you, but Deacon's right—forget her now while you still can. Don't make the mistake he made. It's not fair to her, and it's not fair on you. I don't want to see you go through that, James. And if you did . . ." She shook her head, as if clearing away an ugly thought.

She was scared of what he'd do, he knew it because he'd thought the same thing. After Nicole's death, Deacon had been so broken he'd walked away, not even seeking revenge. He was too distraught to wake up in the morning, let alone hunt down her killers and make them pay. But James was different, and they all knew it. He would hunt down every single one of them, and he would make them, and their entire families, pay. No one would be safe. He didn't want to become that man, but he knew it was inside of him if he was ever so provoked.

"See?" Cami said, holding her hands up. "You know it. If you go down this path, hell will have a new ruler."

James ignored her, checking the flight path.

"I'm going back to sleep, and you should try and get some too. When we land, it's on," James said, closing his eyes again and drifting off into a dark, dreamless slumber.

He remembered her scent, the same scent that filled Dasha's apartment now. He sat quietly on a chair beside the window, looking out onto the street. He'd been waiting for two hours, and he was prepared to wait all night.

"Target entering front lobby," Samuel's voice came through his earpiece.

"Copy," James and Cami repeated.

James looked at his watch, expecting her to walk through the door in three minutes, the time it had taken him. He heard the jostling of keys and with it his body came alive, heightened with anticipation and excitement. He was doing what he was best at, even if it didn't make him a good man.

Her tall silhouette stepped into the apartment, and she paused at the alarm pad. He'd deactivated it, and she knew she wasn't alone.

She turned the lights on and he gave her a sultry smile. He had once shared a bed with Dasha, many years ago, but these days he guessed she'd rather cut off his dick than suck it again.

She masked her shock well, but he knew better. "Liam Smith," she said with her thick Russian accent. As she walked toward him, the split of her dress revealed her upper thigh, and her fingers so subtly lifted it higher, but he wasn't distracted.

"Everyone said you were dead, Liam, but I didn't believe it, not without a body. It's good to see you again." She stopped six feet from him.

"Is it? I think you're lying," James said, raising one eyebrow.

"What do you want, Liam?" She crossed her arms over her chest and James watched her fingers carefully while maintaining eye-contact.

"Information, of course. What else would I be here for?" He smirked and her chest rose with a tightness that told him she was on edge—exactly as he'd intended.

"What do you want to know?"

"I want to know about Escanta," James said, and her eyes flashed with recognition.

"What does a dead man like you want with Escanta?"

"It doesn't matter, Dash. Tell me what you know and I'll leave quietly. If you don't tell me . . . Well, you know how that goes."

She took a step forward. "I can't tell you much, because there isn't much to tell." She took another step forward. "Escanta is a cover-up, for something much bigger. It's small, and it's intended to be a distraction—it's like a plaque on a building wall, a plaque with the wrong business name. You're not looking for Escanta, you're looking for whatever is behind the walls."

"And what is behind the walls?" James asked, not backing down as she leaned forward, cupping his jaw with one hand.

"I don't know," she said.

James saw the metal glisten in the moonlight before he saw her move. He reacted, without hesitation—his mind knew what to do after years of training.

Dasha jumped back, but it was too late—he'd swiped the blade from her fingers and, with one hand, secured her wrists behind her back. He slammed the blade into the flesh of her shoulder joint, hurting her with her own weapon. Dasha was a blade expert, but she relied heavily on it, too heavily—it made her predictable.

His hand covered her mouth, muffling her scream, and he stood up, positioning her on his seat by the window. He took a small, thin rope from his back pocket and secured her to the chair and then stepped back to view the raging anger in her eyes.

"I told you not to lie to me," James said. "And I saw your busy fingers well before you pulled the blade from your sleeve."

Her head tilted forward, the knife in her shoulder sending what James knew to be excruciating bolts of pain through her body.

James put one hand on the knife blade and turned it, butchering a hole in her shoulder cavity. Again he muffled her cry with his hand but he didn't have long now—someone would hear her and alert the police, or worse, her friends.

"If you don't answer my question, the next one will be a full turn. Understood?" James asked.

"What do you want?" Dasha spat at him.

"I want to know who is behind Escanta. Don't tell me you don't know. You've been a busy woman, Dasha, playing both sides of the game and getting into bed with the enemy." Her eyes widened and James laughed. "I might have disappeared, Dash, but do you really think I don't keep tabs on what my friends are up to? Look, I don't care who you're fucking, and I'm not here on behalf of the agency, which you're stealing information from and feeding to your boyfriend. I just want to know about Escanta."

Her breath wheezed in and out and James hoped she wasn't going to pass out before he had what he wanted. *Talk quickly, Dasha.*

"Russians. Escanta is a Russian group. The members change every six months, so that they can't be traced. They collect information, on people like you, and feed it behind the walls."

"Who are they feeding it to, Dasha?"

"I don't know. It's a group"—she coughed—"layers of groups. Behind Escanta is another, and then another, and then another. It's like peeling back a rotting onion. They're bad men, Liam, and even the Mafia doesn't like them. They run in their own circles, and they don't mix with us. The word is that the main group, the ones who control everything, have been running an underground cult with occult practices for hundreds of years. That's all I know, and if you want to find out more, find the head of Escanta. He will be the only one with a link to the next layer."

James clenched his jaw. It was bad news—a mystery of horrors.

"How many in Escanta?"

"I don't know . . . eleven, twelve maybe. You won't find them in Russia, though. Go to Hungary."

"Why Hungary?"

Dasha pressed her lips together, and James turned the knife, watching the blood leak onto the floor like a flowing tap. She was seconds away from unconsciousness.

"Their headquarters are there. That's where the group makes their money, mostly in drug smuggling—heroin."

"Give me a name," James pressed, his grip adjusting on the blade.

"I don't know! I don't know!" Dasha screamed and James knew he'd extracted all he could. And it was time to leave before she attracted any further attention.

"You've been most helpful," James said, smirking.

"Fuck you!" Dasha said as he walked away. "How did you do it, Liam? How did you get out of the agency alive?"

James paused, watching her fight to stay awake, to hear his answer, but it was a battle she was never going to win. Her eyes rolled backward and her head slumped forward.

"I made a deal. Take care, Dash," James said as he moved toward the door. Cami emerged from the adjoining sitting room, where she'd been waiting in the shadows, and they exited wordlessly.

They took the stairs, three at a time until they were in the foyer. Samuel gave them the all clear as they stepped out onto the street but James still did his own surveillance—you could never be too careful.

Cami unlocked the car and they slid in.

"Go," James said, as he set to work removing the second skin that was attached to his fingers—it masked his fingerprints. There would be no police investigation, though, because then Dasha would have to admit what had happened. And that would never happen. Not a single word about tonight would ever leave her lips unless Escanta came for her. That was a risk James should've eliminated by killing her but he couldn't do it, not given their past, not after Paris.

"Samuel, ring it in," James instructed when they were several blocks south of her apartment.

"Consider it done," Samuel said.

By the time the anonymous call was placed and the medic crews reached Dasha, James and Cami would be long gone—like ghosts in the night.

7

MAK ASHWOOD

Thirteen files sat atop one another, like a leaning tower ready to topple. Mak hoped the tower wasn't an omen of how the case would proceed. She prepared for her cases like she had done for her university exams—every detail was meticulously noted, every fact memorized, every explanation analyzed. And she prepared early. There was no last-minute cramming, no pushing of the deadline. And now she had sixteen hours until she had to be in court.

"Kayla," Mak said as her girlfriend answered her phone.

"Hiya, gorgeous. Are you ready? Are you nervous?" Kayla asked.

"All of the above," Mak said.

Kayla was a childhood friend who had also become a lawyer. She'd gone in a different route, specializing in medical litigation, but she still understood.

"You teach those bad boys who's boss, Mak. So, are we going out for our customary pre-trial drink?"

It was a ritual that before either of them had a big case ready for trial, they would go out for a drink. Just one, but one was enough to take the edge off the nerves and ensure a decent night's sleep.

"I'm ready when you are," Mak said.

They confirmed the details, and Mak found herself grinning as she hung up the phone. She locked the files in the cabinet, grabbed her bag, and locked her office behind her. Her bodyguard, one much less interesting than Cami, was waiting for her in the hallway.

"I'm going to The Market, on Essex Street," Mak said.

The past week had been interesting. She had moved apartments, and with the impending trial she was still living in a maze of boxes. It didn't feel like home, and she felt uncomfortable in the space. She hoped it was a temporary measure, and given that she hadn't received any more notes, she felt more confident, more protected.

Kayla was waiting for her when she arrived and had managed to secure a table in the busy cocktail bar. She sat poised like a true lady with her legs crossed and her cheek resting in the palm of her hand. Mak's life hadn't been easy at times, but Kayla's had been worse. She went through a rough patch, got kicked out of school, got hooked on cocaine, but had managed to turn her life around. Luckily she'd never been arrested during those days, otherwise her legal dreams would never have been realized. They'd lost touch briefly but had reconnected when Kayla went into rehab. And they'd spoken nearly every day since.

"I took the liberty of ordering," Kayla said, eyeballing Mak's security.

"I will be stationed by the bar," her bodyguard said and walked off. Mak breathed a sigh of relief.

"How's that going?" Kayla asked with a humored smile.

"Don't get me started. He's driving me nuts. And he's got as much personality as a piece of cardboard."

Kayla burst into laughter, her entire chest shaking as she giggled.

"Anyway," Mak continued, "this is my life for the time being so no point giving it much more thought. Let's talk about something else—anything else, please."

"Well, I've got news . . . I'm going home next week. For a few days, maybe less, maybe more, we'll have to see how it goes."

Mak thought the apprehension in Kayla's voice probably reflected the thoughts in her mind.

"Wow. That is good news, right?" Mak asked.

Going home to see your parents should be no big deal, it should be something you look forward to, but Kayla had barely spoken to her parents in years, let alone seen them. The last time she had been at her parents' house she was sitting on the front doorstep with a duffel bag of belongings—after they'd kicked her out. They had reason: she'd stolen from them, she'd verbally abused them, and she'd caused a scene in front of her younger siblings. Kayla had since rebuilt her life, but Mak guessed Kayla's parents were still hurting.

"It should be, I suppose. I don't know, Mak, I'm terrified to go back there. The memories . . . they're not good." Kayla wet her lips and averted her glistening eyes.

Mak reached across the table and squeezed her arm. "Things are different now. You're different, and you're healthy and successful. Forgiveness is a long road, right? And it's taken a long time for your parents to get to this point, so they wouldn't want you to come home unless they were sure about it."

"I know, and logically it makes sense. But there's still some part of me that is terrified of stepping up to the front door of that home, of not being allowed in again."

"That's not going to happen," Mak said. "When are you going?" She wished she could go with her, but Mak's trial aside, this was something Kayla had to do on her own.

"Next weekend." Kayla dabbed at the corner of her eye. "Please tell me my mascara hasn't smudged. I paid a good price for this water-proof shit."

"You look as beautiful as the moment I walked in." Mak beamed a grin so big she felt it stretch her face.

Kayla scoffed. "Smooth, Mak, smooth. Oh, three o'clock looking fine."

Mak's eyes bulged in surprise: Deacon Thomas.

"Unbelievable," Mak muttered. He sat on one of the couches with a group of four men, and right on cue, as she sat staring at him with her jaw open wide, he looked up.

"Talk to me, Mak," Kayla urged.

"He's the other owner of the security firm, the one handling Jayce Tohmatsu's security."

"The brother of the guy on your flight, correct?" Kayla asked.

"Correct," Mak mumbled. Kayla's eyes crossed to the couch. "He's coming over."

Mak turned toward him. "It's a surprise to see you here," she said.

"Likewise," Deacon said. "I heard your trial starts tomorrow. Good luck." He turned to Kayla, introduced himself, and then turned straight back to Mak.

"How is everything going?" he asked, nodding in the direction of her bodyguard.

Mak shrugged her shoulders. "It appears to be fine, but how would I really know?"

His smile was beautiful and innocent, but Mak thought underneath the *persona* he was nothing of the sort. "Everything is fine," he said. It was a reassurance, and Mak wondered how he knew such things if he was no longer handling her security. Was he watching her too?

"Good to know," she said, looking past him to the group of men on the couch. "Boys' night out?"

"If that's what you want to call it," Deacon said.

"I thought you'd be too busy for a night out," Mak pushed back. She still thought about that meeting and wondered if the excuse they had given her was the truth, or if there was more going on. But perhaps she was overanalyzing it—she did have a lawyer's mind, one that questioned everything.

He smiled at her jab. "Believe it or not, I'm actually working." When she looked down at his glass, he continued, "It's Coke—you can have some if you'd like."

"Thank you, but I'll stick to my martini. How is Cami? She's much better company than the guy you hooked me up with."

Deacon chuckled. "She's good. I'll tell her you said so when I see her next. She'll love the compliment."

"Please do," Mak said, not sure what else to say.

"I'll leave you to it. It was nice to meet you, Kayla, and take care, Mak." His eyes bore a hint of resemblance to his brother's in that moment—in that there was something hiding behind them.

"He seems too lovely to be true," Kayla said, watching him as he walked back to his seat on the couch.

"Doesn't he?" Mak said, swallowing the last of her cocktail.

"Is his brother equally charming?" Kayla asked.

James Thomas seemed to be many things, but charming was not one of them. "*Alluring* is probably a better word," Mak said. "He's less pretty but much more handsome. And he has a certain air about him . . . a certain energy. I barely know him but from what I've observed I think he's very skilled at hiding who he is. I would say there are very few people who truly know him," Mak said, stirring the toothpick around the empty glass. "But sometimes it's not what someone says or does that gives away their secrets. It's what they don't do, right?"

"Hmm," Kayla said thoughtfully.

"Are you done?" Mak asked, looking at Kayla's empty glass. "I should go home and get some rest."

"Yes, I'm done," she said, sliding off the stool. "Good luck tomorrow, girl. You've got this." And there wasn't a tinge of doubt in her voice.

Mak stared at him like she was looking down the barrel of a gun. He didn't flinch, he didn't falter, but he clearly didn't enjoy it. She'd had him on the witness stand for two hours now.

"Mr. Bassetti, when did you immigrate to the United States of America?"

"In 1965."

"And when you immigrated, you did so with your parents, your brother, and your sister. Is that correct?"

"Yes, it is."

"And have any other family members immigrated since then?"

"No."

"So, all of your mother's and father's families remain in Italy. Is that correct?"

"Objection!" Mr. Bassetti's lawyer called. "Seek to relevance?"

"I'm seeking to establish the family dynamic," Mak responded, squaring her shoulders.

"Overruled. Answer the question, Mr. Bassetti."

"Yes, they remain in Italy."

"And in which province do the majority of them reside?" Mak pressed on.

"Objection! Your Honor, his family's location has no relevance to this case."

The judge looked between the two lawyers, paused, and then spoke. "I'll allow it, but make your point, quickly, Mrs. Ashwood."

Mak walked toward the jury, placing one had on the banister. Mak repeated the question.

"They are based in Naples."

Mak's lips teased a smile. "Naples. The base of the Camorra Mafia. Mr. Bassetti, do any of your family members—?"

"Objection!"

"Sustained," the judge ruled.

"No further questions at this time," Mak said, having successfully planted the seed.

"You may step down, Mr. Bassetti. This court is adjourned. We will resume tomorrow at eight a.m."

Mak collected her papers, letting the courtroom empty before she walked into the media circus.

"That was a bold move, bringing up the mafia so early in the game," her assistant prosecutor, Daniel, whispered.

"It's a key aspect of this case. I need it to be front and center in the jurors' minds."

Mak knew it was a risk, but it was a case she had to take risks on. If she played safe, she would lose. As Mak turned to leave, she saw the father of one of the victims still sitting in the pews. His daughter, had she still been alive, would be Mak's age. He was the reason she did what she did. The dead were gone, and it was their surviving loved ones who suffered the most. Mak couldn't bring the victims back, but she could give their families justice. Provided she won. The gravity of his eyes, sunken and sullen in his lined face—it was that look that drove her to bring these broken people some peace.

8

JAMES THOMAS

There were few countries in the world that James had never visited, and Hungary was one of them. Until now.

James and Cami had been in Hungary a week, and they had managed to track down three Escanta members. Each member revealed something different, like pieces of a puzzle, and James thought he now had enough to know who the Escanta leader was, but he was waiting on confirmation from Samuel.

"That looks disgusting," James said.

"It tastes so good," Cami said, her mouth full and bulging with lángos.

"How do they make it?" James asked, drinking his coffee.

"I don't know . . . I guess they fry up the dough and then slather it with sour cream and cheese. Mm-mmm," she said, patting her stomach. "If I die tonight and this is my last meal, at least I'll die happy."

James laughed at her joke. If Samuel gave them the information they wanted, tonight could be a hairy situation. When your career revolved around life and death situations, you learned quickly to adopt a good sense of humor and poke fun at the situation. It was preferable to a nervous breakdown.

"I hope this is our last night here," James said. "I'm anxious to get back to New York."

"Me too. You're starting to annoy the shit out of me," Cami said, laughing. "Seriously, though, I am looking forward to going home, too. In the agency I was a complete nomad, always moving with no real base, and it never bothered me. And now we've been away a little over a week, and I'm already missing my apartment."

A waitress came over to their secluded table and James waited for her to put down the bottle of water and walk away before he responded. "That's because we've created a home in New York—a home that none of us have had for a long time. And in some ways that makes us vulnerable, and predictable, but we can't run forever, and we can't all run together. It's a risk worth taking."

Cami nodded her head. "You know that's the most you've said this trip."

James shrugged his shoulders. "You should travel with Deacon if you want to talk all day long."

She ignored his remark. "You're quieter than you usually are, and that concerns me," Cami said.

"I'm quiet and thoughtful, because I have the Russians on my back."

"If you say so, boss," she said, lifting her sunglasses to wipe her face. It was an unusually hot summer day, and the heat was so dry it felt like it leeched the water from your blood.

Cami didn't look convinced, though, and James wasn't confident in his words either. He was concerned about the Russians, but he was also concerned about his feelings for Mak Ashwood, or rather that he had some semblance of feelings for her. It was definitely not like him.

"Look at the sky," Cami said, and James turned in his seat, looking up. The beautiful blue sky he'd seen an hour ago was now bruised and battered with dark, stormy clouds.

"That's good," James said. "People will stay indoors tonight." *Fewer potential witnesses.*

Cami nodded in agreement and finished the last of her calorie-loaded snack. "Should we make a move in anticipation for the go-ahead?"

"Let's."

They'd been idle now for twenty-four hours since they'd given Samuel their last lead, and James was itching to move, to get some answers.

They walked through the streets, as inconspicuous as two friends, or siblings. They chatted, stopped to take a few photos, acting like tourists, and then continued on. Nothing about them looked out of place, nothing about them appeared dangerous.

James's phone rang and he was relieved to see it was Samuel.

"Are we on?" James asked.

"We're on. He's your guy. I've sent the address to your phone and set up your GPS. Keep in touch," Samuel said.

"Thanks. Will do." James hung up and then checked the address to make sure it was the same one they'd initially identified. It was. This was it—if all went well, tonight he would have the link to the next layer. He would be one step closer.

As soon as the sun melted into the horizon, Cami and James were ready. They had spent the last hour surveying the street and associated apartment block, and, with the building blueprints Samuel had managed to steal from God knows where, they had entry and exit strategies in place.

Cami was to play the key role, and she looked every bit the part. The locks of her brown wig bounced on her shoulders as she walked toward the target's door. Mr. Alberto had a love of women, women he paid for services, and Cami was a special gift from Madame Bella for being her best customer this month. James had balked when he looked over the credit card transactions—Mr. Alberto spent more on prostitutes than James paid himself every month.

James sidled up to the recess in the wall. It wasn't a good hiding spot, this hallway didn't have any, but he doubted Mr. Alberto would keep Cami waiting long.

Cami knocked on the door.

Silence.

She waited patiently and then knocked again.

Silence.

He should've been home, he'd been more than eager to receive his gift when they'd telephoned earlier.

"Samuel, open the door," James said. "Cami, be careful."

"Go," Samuel said and Cami pushed the door open. She leaned in and said, "Mr. Alberto? Mr. Alberto, are you home?"

When she took a step inside, James sprinted down the hallway, following her in. Cami was standing beside the bloody body when he caught up to her.

"Samuel. He's dead," James said, leaning forward to touch Mr. Alberto's body. "An hour, perhaps, given his body temperature. They knew we were coming."

"Fuck it!" Samuel swore and James and Cami looked at each other in surprise. Samuel didn't swear often, and it was almost hilarious when he did. James might have laughed except for the sobering bloody pulp of a man at his feet.

"Two entry wounds and he took a good beating, which I would guess came first. A punishment, perhaps, and then a guarantee that he wouldn't talk," James said, thinking aloud.

"I think you should come home, James. We've got nothing else to go on at the moment. Let Escanta re-group, and then we'll have another shot," Samuel said. "I might be able to dig up something else in the meantime."

The last sentence seemed to be added on as a gift of hope, but James took it anyway. He had nothing else to hold on to at this stage.

"All right, we're going to the airport. Book us flights home," James said, taking one last look at Mr. Alberto.

Damn.

They could have chosen to live anywhere in the world, but James and

Deacon had chosen New York. At the time they'd been on the run for four years—hiding from the agency and their enemies—and no one had been able to find them until Samuel did. Samuel had performed his own disappearing act from the CIA, which James hadn't been aware of at the time, and he'd taken his most valuable asset with him: his skills.

On a crisp, Chicago morning, an unidentified package had arrived by courier. It had no sender details, and it was addressed to *Liam Smith*. Inside the box was a cell phone. The agency found them, or so they'd thought. They grabbed their duffel bags, their only belongings, and were about to run when the phone rang. They looked at it, debating whether to answer it.

If the agency knew where they were, why weren't they banging down the door? Or worse, why weren't they firing bullets through the walls? If they knew where they were, and they wanted to kill them, they'd be dead already. James took a gamble and answered the phone.

Samuel had been busy in his time away from the agency. While James and Deacon had been focused on surviving, Samuel had been building programs and hacking into every database he could find. He'd gathered all of the agency's dirty secrets and created a beautiful, haunting, virtual diary that only he had the key to. That key was a piece of code. It was his way out, his guarantee that they wouldn't come after him, because if he didn't enter the code every so often, this digital vault would explode itself all over the Internet. But he needed someone to tell the agency this, to negotiate his freedom, and not get killed in the process. And who better than *Liam Smith*? And so Liam became the second man with a key.

"Coffee?" Cami said, yawning as she sat behind the wheel, driving them home from the airport, pulling James out of his memories. James rarely drove—he liked to be in a position where he could move fast if they ever came under attack.

The yawn was contagious. "Sounds good. We'll get one for Samuel and Deacon, too. We'll debrief when we arrive and then you should take the rest of the day off," James said.

"You don't need to tell me twice," she said, veering into a parking slot.

James offered to run in—any excuse to stretch his legs again after the long flight—and took his position in a long line of coffee addicts. He looked at the television screen, which was broadcasting the morning news—another terrorism attack, another corrupt government official, a global market crash—it was always a variation of the same. The real news, the news people needed to hear about, was never made public. The dirtier the secret, the deeper it was buried.

James inched forward slowly, but like always, his mind was alert. He was always watching everyone around him—he could tell you how many people were in the store, how many staff were working, where the exits were, where the cameras were—that way of thinking, of assessing every situation he was in, no matter how mundane, was so ingrained in him he doubted he could break it if he wanted to. Which he didn't. It was good to be aware, and it was an advantage to notice things others didn't—it put you one step ahead of the game.

"The court hearing continues today for the triple murder with suggested links to the Italian Mafia. Criminal prosecutor, Makaela Ashwood, declined to comment on the death threats she has allegedly received but she seemed confident and relaxed as she walked into the courthouse this morning."

James stilled, returning his attention to the television. He hadn't been paying attention but he'd heard every word. Footage of Mak entering the courts, which James assumed had been taken earlier this morning, flashed up on the screen.

James was first in line now but he pretended not to notice as he kept his eyes on the bulletin.

"Excuse me? Are you ready to order?"

"Apologies," James said, flashing the woman behind the counter a smile. "I've been following that murder trial."

"Oh, me too! I hope she wins."

"I've been away for a few days. What are these death threats about?" James asked, aware he only had a few seconds—the woman behind him was agitatedly shifting from one foot to the other.

"They haven't said too much yet. Apparently she received a few messages, notes, I think. They didn't say what was written on them."

"Interesting," James said. "Sorry for holding up your line. I'll have four cappuccinos, please."

She waved her hand. "Oh, no problems at all!"

James handed over the money, avoided her flirty eyes, and promptly moved to the side before the lady behind him became violent. Huffing and puffing in agitation was a bit much so early in the morning, and he could only imagine how the rest of her day would pan out.

How did the media find out about the notes? Mak had sworn to secrecy on the notes, so there should only have been four sources: Thomas Security, Mak's new security firm, Mak's old security firm, and the people that sent them. No one else should've known. James's gut feeling told him someone's system had been hacked. And no one had mentioned it to James.

He mulled it over in his mind and then decided not to say anything immediately. He'd wait until the debriefing was done, and if it still hadn't been mentioned, he'd bring it up.

James was surprised to see Mak looking so reassured when her nerves must have been sparking like hot coals. She looked good on the television, very good. She looked beautiful, and he found himself wishing he could see her in the courtroom doing what she did best. Some men were intimidated by strong women, but James was turned on by them, and turned on by this one more than any other he'd ever met.

There were no further news updates on the trial, so with the tray of coffees in his hand, James made his way back to the car.

"Geez, that took a while," Cami said, her eyes on the traffic.

"It was busy," James said, but his mind was occupied on the news bulletin he'd just seen. The more he thought about Mak's case, the more he didn't like it. Something wasn't right—something about those notes was off. They were too cryptic, too vague. It could be the mob's strategy: to scare the hell out of her without it looking like it was coming from them. But say it wasn't from them? Unlikely, but a possibility. Then who else had something to gain? And what else did they have planned?

"Unusually quiet, James." Her words were more warning than concern.

"Yes, Cami, we just got off a long flight, and I didn't sleep. What would you like to chat about?"

Her lips pouted, and he thought she might reprimand him for his snarky attitude, but she didn't. She let this one pass, probably because he almost never took out his emotions on her. James had learned at a very young age to control his temper. A man with a temper made mistakes. A man with a temper was a liability.

They pulled into the underground garage, and James juggled the tray of coffees in one hand and his bag in the other as they rode the elevator up to Samuel's office.

Samuel and Deacon were waiting for them, suitably excited about the coffees. James led the debriefing, recapping everything that had happened in Russia and Hungary, even though Samuel and Deacon had been witness to almost all of it via cameras and earpieces.

"What have you been able to find out about European groups, or cults, with occult practices? The more I think about it the more it concerns me," James said.

Samuel sighed. "It concerns me, too. I've been able to find some data on a Slovenian group that performs black magic, primarily in the form of spells using herbs and alchemy. I don't want to write them off yet, but they don't seem particularly dangerous—the surrounding area has an average crime rate and no ritual deaths have been reported. Additionally, they tend to keep to themselves as far as I can tell.

"Another group in Romania has appeared on my radar. These guys are a little more concerning. Three years ago, two members of this group were arrested for a series of murders and each of the victims received similar wounds. They are evidently in favor of skinning, dismembering and disemboweling their victims. They then wrap them in white sheets and bury them.

"The third group, however, is the most concerning. And I am

assuming this is a group or cult. Romania has a high number of unsolved murder cases, and in a high percentage of those cases, the blood of the victims has been drained, and the number six has been carved into their chest. Make of that what you will, but it points to a cult or ritual killing. I'm going to need some time to work on this group and gather more information," Samuel said.

"Focus on that third group. And research any symbolic significance of the number six," James said.

"Will do," Samuel confirmed, and they all looked at each other, presumably thinking the same thing: this could get ugly.

But with nothing new to add, the debriefing was over.

"So," James said, starting what he knew would be an unpleasant conversation, "I was standing in line to get the coffees, and, much to my surprise, a news bulletin came on, discussing the death threats Mak Ashwood has received. Does anyone want to tell me about this?"

"No," Deacon said with an unwavering stubbornness. "It's under control."

"How is it under control? It looks very not-under-control from my position. Cami? Samuel?" James said, looking at each of them in turn.

Cami diverted her eyes, taking a sip of her coffee and effectively dismissing him.

Samuel appeared to be vacillating in his resolution to withhold information.

James gave him the look, one he rarely had to use, the look that said don't play games.

"Obviously, information was leaked to the press," Samuel said. "I ran some tests to identify whether the leak was the result of someone's system. As it turns out, I couldn't see the trace of a hack, at all. It's not impossible that I've missed it, but it's extremely unlikely. Extremely. I believe that the information was leaked by the source. They want the press to know, but why? I don't know the answer, and it's probably a question better scrutinized by your mind."

Interesting. "So, everyone thought it best not to tell me?" James asked, looking directly at Deacon.

"Hey, you said you wanted to be involved as little as possible. And, now that you do know, what are you going to do about it? Nothing. So why does it matter? All it will do is put that girl back in your mind, and we all know that's a fucking bad idea."

James sat silently for a minute, thinking through the strategy forming in his mind. "Actually, you're right—I'm not going to do anything about it," he said to Deacon. "But you are."

9

JAMES THOMAS

James watched a miniature version of Deacon walk down a dark alley via one of Samuel's surveillance screens. Samuel had hacked into the camera system Mak's new security contract had installed, and James had multiple views of the streets surrounding her office building, the lobby, the floor she worked on, and her actual office.

"Confirm. Two ghosts identified," Deacon said. His voice was being transmitted via his earpiece and played on the speakers in Samuel's office.

Deacon had been loitering around Mak's office, scoping out the surveillance and also testing her external security. They had failed to identify Deacon, which wasn't necessarily a good start but his brother was skilled at slipping into and out of places unseen.

"Enter via the basement," James said, and Samuel nodded his head in agreement.

James watched Deacon move along the east wall, jiggling the windows to see if any were unlocked. Unlikely, but definitely possible. James wished he were the one on-site, testing Mak's security, but it was much better if Deacon did it. As much as she didn't leave his thoughts, he knew engaging with her was a bad idea—it would only make him want something he couldn't have. He would stay away, and spare them both some pain.

Deacon returned to the window in the center of the building—the largest window. He pulled a round disk from his back pocket and stuck it on the center of the glass pane. James noted the time as Deacon pushed the activation button. Within seconds the glass silently crumbled into millions of glistening fragments that looked as innocent as spilled sugar but James knew could cut like razors. Carefully, Deacon climbed through and into the basement of Mak's office building.

Samuel hadn't been able to retrieve a floor plan of the basement —it was a very old building—but Deacon knew the direction of the stairwell. He would have to use his night scope to guide him without turning on the lights, but James estimated it should only take about two minutes for him to reappear on their screens.

"Door locked," Deacon said, keeping in communication—because even the most basic communication during an operation was paramount to its success.

Seven seconds later Deacon spoke again. *"Moving."*

James looked at the camera view of Mak's office. She was at her desk, which was covered in manila folders. James assumed they were notes related to her case.

"Stairwell," Deacon said, confirming his location.

James watched as Mak rubbed her eyes and then stood up from her desk, picking up her coffee mug on her way out. James' eyes flickered to the layout of her floor. The kitchen was located right next to the stairwell.

"Seventh floor."

"Hold," James said, watching Mak walk straight past the door he knew Deacon was standing behind. James watched as she made a cup of coffee.

"Target in the kitchen adjacent to stairwell. Move," James said. He didn't bother to tell Deacon to move quietly—that would've been a redundant order: Deacon could move like a phantom.

James kept his eyes on the surveillance screen of the kitchen and watched as Deacon moved through the screens toward Mak's office. James could only see two other of Mak's colleagues still working in their cubicles and that was good news for Deacon.

The bodyguard outside Mak's office answered his phone, and James wondered if Deacon had been picked up already. But, the bodyguard quickly hung up and his attention was absorbed by something on his phone.

"Now," James said.

Deacon was light on his feet—a silent assailant—and although Mak's bodyguard had only been distracted by his phone for a few seconds, it gave Deacon the element of surprise. By the time the bodyguard saw him, it was too late—Deacon had a pre-prepared syringe jammed in the bodyguard's neck.

The man flinched, gurgled, and then collapsed into Deacon's arms.

"Fucking heavy bastard," Deacon said, and James and Samuel smiled as they watched Deacon haul the man into an unattended cubicle and tuck him under the desk.

"Hold," James said. "Target approaching."

Mak was returning to her office, strangely without her mug. *What is she doing?* James watched her as she neared the cubicle Deacon was hiding in.

James was silent now. Deacon would be able to hear her footsteps, and he knew what to do next. When she was two steps past the cubicle, Deacon grabbed Mak from behind. His left hand went straight to her mouth, and his right hand crossed over the front of her body, pinning her arms down and her back to his chest.

"I'm not going to hurt you, I promise. Walk toward your office," Deacon said.

Mak didn't move.

"Mak, you're okay. Move, one foot in front of the other."

She remained as stationary as a signpost but James watched as Deacon gently guided her forward. She was so petite, so slight, and would be so easy to maneuver.

They stepped over the threshold of her office and James's eyes flickered to the screen with the best view.

"Mak, I'm going to take my hand away if you promise not to scream."

Her head nodded stiffly and James felt bad that she was terrified, but there was no way to truly test her security without surprising her, too.

Deacon withdrew his hand and with it she seemed to let go of the breath she'd been holding. Her body fell forward, most likely due to the release of adrenaline, and she gulped in air like he'd been choking her. James watched as Deacon leaned behind him and closed the door. Mak struggled against his arm so he let her go completely.

She turned to face him, taking two large steps back. Her eyes blazed with anger when she saw him. *"What the fuck?"* she yelled, and Deacon put his index finger over his lips.

Samuel chuckled next to James. "Here we go," Samuel said.

Mak glared at Deacon, unwavering in her fury. *"Are you crazy? Are you trying to give me a heart attack?"* She balled her hands on her hips and even on the camera she looked ferocious despite her slight stature.

Deacon closed the blinds of her window, giving her a few seconds to calm down before he spoke.

James checked his watch again, noting the time.

"I wanted to test your security," Deacon said.

Mak didn't look impressed. *"And you couldn't think of another way?"* She shook her head, seeming to clear her muddled thoughts. *"Wait . . . What are you even doing here? Where is—?"*

Deacon stopped her, blocking her from opening the blinds.

"He's taking a nap," Deacon said.

"What do you mean he's taking a nap?" she asked, almost growling at him.

James felt his lips turn up in a slight smile as he watched the scene unfold.

"He'll be fine in the morning. He'll have the best sleep of his life," Deacon said casually.

"You . . . I . . ." She put her palm to her forehead, clearly over-whelmed at the situation. *"You can't do that! Where is he?"*

"Under the desk in the cubicle three rows to your left."

She rubbed her fingers over her lips. *"Holy shit,"* she said. *"I'm a lawyer—you do realize that, right?"*

"Yes, we're all too aware of that, Mak," Deacon said, sitting down in the chair opposite her desk. *"Take a seat before you fall over."* She sat down on the edge of the desk like on autopilot, definitely still in shock.

Deacon sat silently, and James assumed he was giving her some time for the shock to wear off. Until it had, James knew nothing that came out of Deacon's mouth was going to help.

Mak looked at him now, really looked at him—staring him down like she was about to interrogate him.

"How mad are you?" Deacon asked.

"Furiously mad."

She rested the palms of her hands on the edge of the desk, letting her thin fingers hang over. James looked at the ring on her finger, wondering again if it was her wedding band.

She was quiet for a minute. *"So what's the plan now, mastermind?"* Mak asked curtly.

"We wait," Deacon said, clasping his hands in his lap.

"For what?" she said, looking around.

"For how long it takes them to realize there's been a security breach," Deacon said.

It had already been far too long.

"Why are you testing them? It's been several weeks since my handover," Mak said.

James could tell, as she began to regain some of her composure, that the shock was wearing off.

"We said that we would make sure you were safe. This is part of that; it doesn't end at handover. You should be prepared, though, because they weren't expecting this, and they aren't going to be impressed when they realize what I've done."

She scoffed. *"No, I can't imagine they will be. Holy hell."*

"Want to place a bet on how long it will take them to realize?" Samuel asked, looking across the table at James.

An inappropriate laugh rumbled in James's throat. Samuel loved to gamble—on anything. "I'm scared to do that. My gut feeling is it's going to take them a while, but they should already be on it."

Samuel started typing on his laptop screen and James returned his full attention to the camera screens.

"I've been here for long enough that they should've banged down the door by now. They're not doing their job," Deacon said. *"So, how is the trial going?"*

She raised one eyebrow incredulously. *"You want to talk about the trial?"*

Deacon shrugged his shoulders. *"Might as well, since we've got a few minutes to pass."*

She looked a little flabbergasted. *"It's going well, I suppose. It's hard to know. It's a tough jury—they don't give a lot away. A lot like you."* Her eyes challenged Deacon.

"Me? I let my guard down, but only with those I trust."

"And who do you trust?"

James noted how Mak had effectively turned the tables so Deacon was the one answering the questions. Mak always asked a lot of questions, and James liked that about her. She was interested, and she was interesting.

"There're only three people in this world I completely trust," Deacon said.

"That's not very many."

"It's enough. How many do you trust, Mak?"

She thought it over. *"More than three,"* she said with a lighter voice.

James was confident the shock had worn off now—it was always a good strategy to divert the conversation away from the situation.

"Can I ask you a personal question?" Deacon asked.

James's eyes flickered to Samuel's but he simply shrugged his shoulders, indicating he had no idea where this conversation was going either.

James watched Mak closely now.

"*You can ask it, but I don't know if I will answer it,*" she said.

"*Fair enough,*" Deacon said. "*I read the report, which detailed your husband's disappearance. Why haven't you sought to have him declared deceased?*"

It was the question that James, Samuel, and Deacon had all asked. Did she have a reason to believe he was coming home? A reason that wasn't on paper, something that wasn't in a report. Had someone made contact with her and she'd never told anyone about it?

She looked at the floor, crossing her legs. James didn't think she was going to answer but she did.

"*I don't need a piece of paper to tell me he's dead,*" she finally said.

"Well, mystery solved," Samuel said to James.

James nodded his head but didn't comment. It was the answer he'd wanted to hear, for several different reasons—one of which he didn't want to admit.

Deacon pressed her further. "*Most people want closure when a loved one goes missing, especially after so many years.*"

"*Probably. And I guess I would've if I'd met someone I was serious about, but things haven't worked out that way, so it doesn't matter to me if I am legally married or not—I know my husband's not coming home.*"

Deacon nodded his head. "*I understand.*"

James checked his watch again, almost in unison with his brother. And as if right on cue, a car screeched to a stop in front of the building and two men jumped out.

"Approaching," James said.

"*How much trouble are they in?*" Mak asked Deacon, and James thought the grin on her face was adorable.

Deacon chuckled. "*A lot. We need to discuss your security contract. Obviously, there's an issue here. When we handed over, we gave them specific requirements that we wanted in place. They have done that, but it doesn't mean that they're monitoring you properly. At Thomas Security we set up a lot of systems—'trip codes' as we call them. Basically, systems or factors that are automatically monitored together and if something changes in the system, it sends a message to our monitoring team and they investi-*"

gate. For example, your bodyguard who's taking a nap—his tracker would alert that his pulse rate has dropped significantly, considering what I injected him with, and that would trigger an alert. We'd actually have two bodyguards with you, but even if we didn't we would've tried to call him, and obviously he wouldn't answer, so we'd check the cameras and find out what's going on. That should all take seconds, not fifteen minutes."

"You recommended them," Mak said.

"I know, and that's why I'm testing them. I think given their massive failure tonight, you should terminate the contract, and we'll look after you," Deacon said.

"Did you find some resources overnight?" She crossed her arms over her chest, but her voice had a hint of playfulness.

Deacon ignored the jab. *"Circumstances change every day, Mak."*

"You didn't answer the question, Deacon."

"Yes, then, we found some resources overnight," Deacon said, grinning. *"The choice is yours, Mak."*

James watched as the two men from Mak's security firm ran down the hallway toward her office.

Deacon must have heard them approaching because he said, *"This is going to get ugly."*

The door flung open and two men burst in with guns loaded.

"Mercy, mercy," Deacon said, holding his hands up in surrender. He turned to face the men.

The two men looked at each other, but kept their guns poised.

"What the hell are you playing at, Thomas?" one of the men asked.

"I thought I'd perform a security test. We referred Mak Ashwood to you, provided certain protocols, and systems were put in place. You have failed on almost every one of them. What do you have to say about that?"

They didn't answer.

"Where is Ren?"

"If you're talking about Mak's bodyguard," Deacon said, *"he's taking a nap under a cubicle desk, three rows down."*

Their eyes blazed and one of the men gestured to the other to go and check.

"Do you think this is funny, Thomas?"

That's the wrong question to ask. Deacon was passionate about their business and genuinely cared about all of their clients. It wasn't just an alternative lifestyle to their past, he loved what he did now, and James thought that perhaps by protecting other people, Deacon thought he could somehow atone his soul—just a fraction—for Nicole's death.

Deacon let his true feelings show. *"Funny? No, I don't think it's funny at all. You failed to protect her. You gave me fifteen minutes to break into this building and slit her throat, and all I needed was two-and-a-half minutes and I had her in my arms. Do you think that's funny?"*

"I didn't set the systems up," he rebutted.

"I don't give a fuck who did. At the end of the day, you failed and we will never refer a client to you again. And we will make sure that our contacts know exactly what happened here tonight."

The boutique security industry was a well-connected group, and James knew he realized what that meant to their future.

The second man came back into Mak's office. *"He's alive, but unconscious."*

The man, clearly wearing the pants in this duo, nodded. *"Well, you've made your point. I'll personally ensure she's safe from here."*

Deacon shook his head and then turned to Mak. *"Write a letter terminating your contract and sign it. He can take it back to his boss."*

"Is that your definition of a choice?" she questioned, remaining stationary on the edge of her desk.

James bit his lip, amused at Deacon's slip-up.

Deacon smiled. *"I apologize,"* he said. *"Mak, would you like to stay with these useless guys, or would you like Thomas Security to handle your case from this evening forward?"*

She shook her head, and then stood up and moved to the back of her desk. She typed out a letter on her computer, printed and signed it, sealed it in an envelope and handed it to the man in charge.

"Please pass this on. I will also email a copy, just to make sure it gets there," she said and it was the first time James had seen her show any bitterness at her lack of protection.

The man took the envelope, looked back at Deacon, and then

spoke to his colleague. *"Call the guys. We're going to need help getting Ren out of here."*

Deacon stood up. *"That's all for tonight,"* he said, glaring at the men as he closed the door behind them.

"Are they going to sue you for drugging Ren?" Mak asked.

"They might threaten it, but I'll make a deal with them," Deacon said.

"A deal, huh? What kind of deal?"

"I might tell them I'll keep quiet about what happened here tonight, if they don't sue me."

James smiled, not concerned at all about the potential lawsuit—their boss knew better than to even try such a move.

"I see . . . How often do you make these kinds of deals?" Mak asked.

Deacon ignored her question. *"Now, if you want to stay here and keep working, I'll step outside and resume your bodyguard duties until an arrangement is made. Or, I can take you home. We're going to need access to your apartment tonight anyway."*

"What do you need to do in my apartment?" Mak asked.

"Install a new security system," Deacon said, leaning against the wall.

Mak appeared to groan. *"Okay, I'll finish my work at home while that's being done,"* she said, turning off her computer and tidying her desk. She picked up a bag that looked like it weighed more than she did, and Deacon moved forward to take it from her.

James watched as Deacon escorted Mak out of the building and into his car. James stood and grabbed the black bag by his feet, already prepared in the event tonight unfolded exactly as it had.

He had an install to do.

10

MAK ASHWOOD

Mak stole inquisitive peeks at Deacon Thomas as he drove her home. Tonight had been a bouquet of surprises, and she could never have anticipated it turning out the way it had. He'd thrown her for a loop, and then spun her until she was dizzy. Who were the Thomas brothers?

"Are you okay?" Deacon asked, looking across at her.

"Yes, I was just recapping what happened tonight. It's been a bit of a surprise."

He turned back to the road, but she could still see his grin. He was definitely pretty, the kind of man who would be on a poster hung in the bedroom of a twelve-year-old girl.

"I know, I'm sorry. Sometimes it's like that with us. Just ask Jayce," Deacon said with a slight laugh. "We're not conventional, Mak, and we don't follow all of the rules. We can't, and won't, always justify our actions but I promise you can trust us."

Mak wondered what went on behind the scenes at Thomas Security, and if she really wanted to know the truth.

"How can I trust you if you can't tell me certain things?"

"Because our actions will prove that you can trust us, and every move we make will have your best intentions at heart," Deacon said.

"Is this how it is with all of your clients?"

"Yes, all of them, with no exceptions. It drives them crazy some-times—and it will drive you crazy at some point—but our methods work and our clients know it," Deacon said.

"How many clients do you have?" Mak asked.

He turned to her with a smile. "Just the right amount, Mak."

"Why don't you grow the business further?"

"Because security is a high-risk game, and quality control is imperative. We need to be able to tightly oversee all aspects of our business, and we can't do that if it grows too big."

"And who is 'we'? Who runs Thomas Security?"

"James and I, primarily. Of course we have managers, like every other business, but we are the two owners, as such. I know what you're doing . . ." Deacon said.

Mak played the innocent card. "And what is that?"

Deacon chuckled. "You're asking me questions that you know I'm going to evade, but you're not so much interested in my answers as you are trying to read me, right?"

"I'm just interested in the company that is pledging to protect me," Mak said, tapping her fingers on her knee.

Deacon pulled into the underground garage and used a remote to open it.

"How did you get that?" Mak asked.

"That's none of your concern," he said, grinning like a mischie-vous child. "Don't get out until I open the door for you."

Deacon exited the car and a few seconds later the trunk opened. Mak turned to see him lifting the strap of her bag over his shoulder. She picked up her handbag that was sitting by her feet, waiting for him to open her door. Mak peered out the windows, looking for anything sinister, but in her opinion nothing, or no one, looked out of place.

Deacon opened the car door. "Let's rock 'n roll."

Mak noticed he had a bag over each shoulder—one of them she didn't recognize.

"Are you staying over?" she asked. She meant it as a joke, but as soon as the words left her mouth she regretted them.

A broad, lopsided grin formed on his pink lips. "Definitely not," he said, taking her hand to help her out of the car.

They rode the elevator up to her floor and Mak opened the apartment, turning on the lights.

Deacon stopped, looking at her living room. "Why weren't packers organized? They should've done everything for you."

Mak moved through the mini skyscraper of cardboard boxes she had yet to unpack and put her bag down on the dining table. "They offered, but I declined."

His eyes looked up slightly, like he was thinking something through. "Okay," he said. "As long as they offered."

Mak nodded her head. She had declined to have them moved because she didn't like people going through her things. She didn't want someone she barely knew to go through her belongings, let alone pack her lingerie, or the naughty drawer of her bedside table—how embarrassing.

"Where would you like this?" Deacon asked, slipping her briefcase off his shoulder.

"Oh, thanks, you can just put it here on the table," Mak said. She moved her handbag over, making space for the larger briefcase. Most of her files were electronic, but Mak still liked to handwrite certain notes and print reports. And it was surprising how quickly the weight added up.

He put it down on the table and appeared to take another quick assessment of her apartment. "We're going to strip the surveillance and put in our own system; it shouldn't take longer than an hour. You can get on with your work, or if you're tired we'll do your bedroom first so that you can get some rest. We'll lock up before we leave, and security will be stationed outside all night."

The apartment door opened and James Thomas walked in.

Their eyes locked just like they had the first time they'd seen each other. This time she wasn't scared of him, however, but she still didn't think he was an innocent man.

"Hi, Mak," he said, shaking her hand. Her skin tingled, and she felt her pulse increase as their hands connected.

"I'm sorry about what happened tonight," James said. "We'll make sure all involved are dealt with accordingly."

"Thank you," Mak said, noticing her voice was throatier than normal.

James looked away, almost too quickly, and his eyes traveled over the apartment. "Were you planning to move again?"

"I've only unpacked a few of the things I need. I'll do the rest when the trial is over," Mak said, leaning her hip against the table.

"Okay," he said, mirroring his brother's comment. He looked to Deacon. "Let's get started."

James unzipped the bag he had brought in with him, which looked identical to Deacon's, and pulled out a smaller bag that made a rustling noise as he put it down on the table. He pulled out a folded piece of paper from his back pocket and handed it to his brother.

Deacon looked at it for a minute or so, and then looked up at the ceiling. "Good," he said, not discussing any details.

And neither showed Mak what was on that piece of paper.

"Mak, you can do whatever you need to do. We'll be as quick as possible," James said gently—a polite dismissal, of sorts.

"What's that?" Mak said, eyeballing the paper Deacon passed back to James.

"It's a security plan," James said, folding it back up and putting it in his pocket.

"Can I see it?"

"It's better if you don't," James said, not looking at her.

"Why is that?" Mak questioned.

"Because, if you don't know where the cameras are, and how we are monitoring you, then it's easier to forget that you're under surveillance. It's for your benefit, not ours. It's the same with all of clients—none of them see the security plan," James said, pulling what looked like hardware tools from his bag.

"How often will you look at the cameras?" Mak said.

"We, personally, won't be looking at them at all. The surveillance team will check them from time to time, but they are used more as a double-check if another alert gets triggered. We don't have someone sitting and watching your every move. At this stage, with this level of security, your life should continue as normal. With the exclusion of your bodyguard, you should forget we exist," he said, finally raising his eyes to look at her. It was like a warning, a plea.

"I'd still like to see it," Mak said.

They were at a standoff, and Deacon was the first to speak. "Mak, don't make this more difficult on yourself than it has to be. People become very uncomfortable in their own home if they think too much about the security. Just leave us to it."

"I'll start in the ceiling," James said, not giving her the plan and not continuing the discussion. He lifted his sweater over his head, and his black T-shirt rode up his waist, revealing a rippled abdomen.

Mak's cheeks blushed, and she moved toward the kitchen—security plan forgotten. She opened the door to the refrigerator, pretending to look for something to eat, but really she was letting the icy air cool the heat in her cheeks.

Christ.

A moment later she closed the refrigerator door. There was only so long she could pretend to be looking for a snack because if they looked inside they would realize it was empty. Mak didn't cook, and she barely ate in her apartment. She had two bottles of champagne, a block of cheese, a container of milk and a couple apples—hardly a menu to justify a long deliberation.

She leaned against the counter, watching the two brothers. Deacon handed James a box, which marvelously pulled out into a mini stepladder. He stepped up onto the top rung and, with his fingertips, lifted the ceiling panel to reveal a manhole. He slid the panel to the side, and then with a hand on each edge of the opening, hauled himself upward and into the ceiling cavity. He did it so easily, a result of his sheer body strength.

Mak's apartment door opened again, and this time Cami walked in.

"Hello, again," Cami said brightly, spotting Mak in the kitchen. "You've had quite the night, huh?"

Mak scoffed. "It's been interesting, that's for sure."

"Things are always interesting when these two are involved," she said. "So, I'm going to be your new bodyguard, starting tomorrow."

"Good. That other guy was a bore and a half," Mak said, taking an apple from the fridge, offering one to Cami at the same time.

Cami's eyes peeked behind Mak's body. She grinned. "No, thanks, I wouldn't want to steal half your food supply," she joked.

"I don't eat at home, I'm not even home often," Mak explained. When she had a big trial, she spent most of her time in her office. And when she didn't, she spent most of her time out with friends and family.

"You're lucky," Cami said without elaborating further. "Alrighty, then, I'm going to help these boys so we can get out of here and leave you in peace. We'll have two security guys stationed outside your door tonight, another in the lobby and some more outside. And then I'll be back in the morning. What time do you want to be at the office?"

Mak mentally ran through her day tomorrow. "Six thirty."

"Perfect, I'll be here a half hour before," she said with a nod of her head and then walked to stand beside Deacon.

Cami said something to him, something Mak couldn't hear, and he shrugged his shoulders.

Mak looked around her, unsure what to do now. She really just wanted to shower and go to bed. Instead, she picked up a folder of notes and dropped them onto her bed. She kicked off her shoes, climbed up onto the bed, and settled in for an hour of review work.

11

JAMES THOMAS

"Family meeting," Deacon said as they exited Mak's building.

"Why?" James asked. He'd stuck to the plan all night—the plan Deacon had approved before he left for Mak's office.

"Because I saw the way you looked at her when you walked in, and now I'm questioning your motives again," Deacon said with glaring eyes.

James threw his bag in the trunk. "Fine, I'll meet you in Samuel's office," he said, not wanting to get into this conversation now.

Family meetings always consisted of their party of four, and they were always held in Samuel's office because he was the Switzerland equivalent—he never took sides.

James unlocked his car and got into the driver's seat. He took one last look at Mak's apartment, at the window he now knew was the window to her bedroom. The light was on, but he doubted it would be for long. She'd seemed tired, and they'd worked as fast as they could and did the install in half the usual time. But she was in the middle of a huge trial, and she didn't need the massive distractions they had created tonight, but he was not going to leave her unprotected. A distraction tonight was a small price to pay to avoid massive turmoil in the future.

James drove home, his breath the only sound in the car. He never used the radio—it disguised any noise he might need to hear.

When he reached Thomas Security he pulled into his designated parking bay. His car was the final link in the chain of black sedan's lining the parking lot wall.

Thomas Security had contracted with a luxury manufacturer to design a custom range of armored vehicles for them—the process a highlight of Deacon's life—but James was not partial to any one brand; he simply wanted whatever was best.

James took their private elevator up to Samuel's office, where his little family was waiting. He took his seat, waiting for Deacon to voice his concerns.

"I want the honest truth about your feelings for Mak," Deacon asked.

"She needs to be protected," James said. "I don't like that information was leaked to the media, and neither do you, so you can stop pretending that didn't bother you. I was wrong about my previous decision not to take her as a client, and since we referred them to her, if something would have happened to her, that would have been very bad for Thomas Security." James folded his hands on the table.

Deacon shook his head and he ground his lip between his teeth. "I don't believe that's the only reason."

"Look, I'm not going to deny I'm attracted to her, but that's where it will end. I have no intention to pursue her. She's a client now, and that's it. You will manage her security and I'll oversee it—exactly how it should've been in the first place."

"Can you stay out of it?" Deacon asked, raising his eyebrows.

"Yes," James responded, hoping he wasn't lying to his brother.

"I've never seen that look in your eyes," Deacon responded.

"That's because you rarely see me look at a woman."

"Exactly. Because you were the one who encouraged that rule, the one who has always lived by the opinion that it's better to not get into relationships at all because it only ends badly. Having her as a client is like dangling chocolate in front of someone on a diet. Sooner or later they will give in. You'll give in, and I promise you, it's not going to end well."

"You were fine with this plan a few hours ago," James said.

"Yeah, that was before I saw lust in your eyes. Paris has changed you, whether you want to admit it or not. I don't know what you're looking for with her, or even if you know, but the only thing that's going to heal what happened is time. You can't fill the void of losing your—"

"I didn't lose anything," James said. "I killed him."

"Stop," Cami said, shaking her head gently. "It was an accident, James. Don't say it like that."

"I say it like that because it's the truth—accident or not, he's dead."

"I just wish you would talk to us," Deacon said. "I wish I knew what was going on inside your head."

"How much talking did you do after Nicole's death?" James asked. He didn't want to bring up Nicole, but there was no better way to make the point.

Deacon looked away, grinding his teeth, but after a few seconds he sighed in resignation. "Okay," Deacon said, turning over his empty hands in a gesture indicating he was giving up.

Deacon hadn't wanted to talk about Nicole, and even now rarely did, and James didn't want to talk about Paris.

"Look," Cami said, "she's our client, and we're going to protect her as we do any other client. And seeing as this conversation is going nowhere, I'm going to bed because I've got to be back at Mak's early." She put her hands flat on the table, looked at each of them, and when there were no objections she stood up and left.

"I'm going, too," Deacon said, briefly nodding goodbye to James and Samuel.

When the door closed, James sighed and looked at Samuel.

"They're concerned. And so am I," Samuel said.

"Do you think we're making a mistake taking her on as a client?" James asked.

"Regarding your personal feelings, yes, I do—I agree with

Deacon. But from a security angle, no, because I didn't like her security from the start. I'm not sure how much danger she's actually in, though. I do think they're trying to scare her more than anything."

"Deacon is really upset by this," James said.

"Well, he has a right to be. You should not get involved with her, and you know it—*especially* while you're being hunted by Escanta," Samuel said. "Deacon never dealt with Nicole's death, and I think this is bringing up all those feelings again. It's probably going to force him to deal with the demons he's buried for so long, and it's probably going to get uglier before it gets better. He's resisting, and he's going to push back at you because he so desperately doesn't want to deal with the pain that burdens him. Be patient with him, James."

"I will," James said thoughtfully.

When James had found Deacon in that warehouse, he'd taken almost a year to physically recover from his injuries, even with intensive rehabilitation. But he'd never recovered emotionally—they had beaten his soul, searing it to its core.

They were a quiet for a few seconds.

"Can you please display Mak's surveillance on the screens?" James asked.

Samuel pressed a couple buttons and then the wall transformed into a series of images, the result of their install. All of the lights were off in her apartment, and he could see her small body tucked up in bed.

James assessed the surveillance, checking for any blind spots. "Good," he said, and Samuel turned it off.

"So, I wasn't going to say anything, but I might as well now," Samuel said. "You know how I love a mystery, so I've been doing a little digging around on Mak's husband. He was quite the ambitious young man. Started his first company at seventeen, bankrolled by investors. By the time he was nineteen he was a multi-millionaire— without including the money in the offshore accounts. But that's not the interesting part—this is: Around when he turned eighteen, he began traveling—a lot. Mostly in Europe. I've put together a file on his whereabouts over this time, up until the point he went missing.

"He booked the travel through his business, but I'm finding it hard to track any movement from the time he landed on those trips. I have records of his plane tickets, but then nothing—I can't find any hotel bookings, no car rental records. It's like he ceased to exist when he landed. Interesting, don't you think?" Samuel looked proud and intrigued.

"Very," James agreed. "What are the chances that someone like you could delete that kind of information?"

"It's possible, but I don't think that's what happened. I think once he landed he became someone else—used an alias. Or several."

"And this guy had no military training, right? No agency, no Special Forces?" James asked.

"Nope. So if he did assume an alias, he had help," Samuel said.

"So who was helping him?"

"That's the mystery, isn't it?"

"Do you think anything about this connects with Mak's case?" James asked.

Samuel sighed. "I really don't. He disappeared thirteen years ago, so if whoever killed him off wanted something, they would've come for her. It's not like she's been hiding—she has stayed in Manhattan the entire time and taken on increasingly higher-profile cases. If they haven't come for her before, we'd say at this point she's statistically safe, right?"

"Right," James said. "But you know what I think of 'statistically safe.' I agree, though, it doesn't make sense, particularly given that she's never touched that money."

Samuel yawned. "I'm not looking into it because I'm concerned from a security angle, I just want to know what happened to him."

"I hate to admit it, but I do, too. Keep looking into it when you have spare time," James told him, smiling now. Samuel never had spare time, but somehow he managed to squeeze in these little mysteries—they were Samuel's version of a hobby.

"Can you please send me all of the intelligence for Mak's case and her husband's? I want to look over it myself," James said.

"I'll send it to you in the morning. You need to sleep, James.

You've had a busy few weeks, and Cami said you barely slept on the flight home. If you want to help this woman, the best thing you can do is be alert and ready when she is awake and moving about. You're no good to her if you're tired and making mistakes. Review it tomorrow, and we'll catch up again in the evening."

"Okay, Dad," James joked. Samuel was sometimes more like a father than a friend, and sometimes he needed that.

~

Samuel delivered, and James spent the entire next day reviewing the intelligence they'd gathered on Mak and her missing husband. His disappearance was interesting, absolutely, but nothing outwardly concerning.

And since his disappearance, Mak had lived an ordinary, albeit successful life. The notes had only started when she was deep into this case, and the mob certainly wasn't against intimidating people—it was a daily habit for them. But something didn't sit well with James, an ominous sense of something not quite right but not tangible either. He'd had these feelings before, and he'd usually been right. He hoped he was wrong on this occasion.

But if he was wrong, something else occurred to him. The case would be over soon, a few weeks tops, perhaps. And then she'd probably have no need for his company's services, or at the very most she'd have minimum security like Jayce—security he wasn't involved in at all. She might come back to them, when she took another high-profile case, and James thought perhaps the universe was going to bring her in and out of his life, dangling her in front of him. Maybe this sense of longing for something he couldn't have was his punishment for all of the bad things he'd done in his life.

The door to his office swung open and Deacon walked in.

"You're still here," Deacon said, sitting down opposite James.

"Looking over client reports," James said, explaining why he was still in his office at midnight on a Friday night.

"Looking over Mak Ashwood's file?" Deacon rocked the chair back so that it balanced on its two hind legs.

"Yes," James said. He didn't want to lie to Deacon—it wouldn't help the situation.

"Well, we might as well talk about the case, seeing as we're handling it now," Deacon said.

"After reviewing the intelligence, I'm not sure how much of a case there is."

Deacon paused. "You said you thought this was going to get complicated . . ."

"Yeah," James said. "The mob is unpredictable, so who knows what they have planned, but as long as we protect her properly she should be fine. I thought the circumstances around her husband going missing were weird, but after looking at the additional details Samuel's found . . . I think he was doing some dirty business and got in over his head. It happens all the time."

Deacon's eyes narrowed. "So why do you have that look on your face?"

"I just have a bad feeling about those notes, the scrolls, but I don't know why. I can't find anything to justify my anxiety."

Deacon sighed, letting the chair float down on all fours. "I don't want to suggest this, because I want you to forget all about her, but maybe we should go and do some surveillance tonight? Cami checked in, advising she was taking her to a cocktail bar downtown. We'll go and have a look . . . It might put your mind at ease?"

James tapped his finger on his chin.

"Look, I'd suggest it's better if I do it on my own," Deacon said, "but I know you better than that, and how you like to double-check things, so let's just go and get it over with."

James considered it. They had nothing else pressing to do, and it would put his mind at ease.

"Okay, let's do it," James said, pushing his chair back.

The men checked in with Samuel and then went down to the parking lot. Deacon drove, and although the tension between them was unresolved, it felt less strangling when they worked together.

Deacon had never been under James's command in either Delta Force or the agency—Deacon had been a Ranger. But they'd worked together on a joint mission, the last mission either of them went on— the mission that changed everything. When you've seen the things they had, it bonded you in a way that could not be broken. Blistering tragedy could tie souls together for eternity.

"How are Cami and Mak getting along?" James asked.

"Good, I think. Cami hasn't said anything, and Mak seems comfortable." Deacon's eyes left the road only to check the mirrors.

"Good," James said. He wanted Cami partnered with Mak because she was their best, besides himself or Deacon.

"You need to be very careful around her," Deacon said. "And I'm not saying that because of what you so obviously feel for her. But she asks questions, a lot of them, and then you can almost see her turning the information over in her mind. She's not unlike us in that she's been trained to question everything—but she does it the right way, the legal way. Behind that pretty, innocent face of hers, that mind is working, and if you're not careful, she'll piece together much more than you want her to."

"I know," James said. Sometimes it was the way she looked at him after he answered one of her many questions—she paused, holding his gaze, tethering his mind like she was drawing further data from it. It was dangerous.

They arrived at the bar and Deacon pulled up around the corner.

"What's the plan?" James asked, letting Deacon call the shots tonight.

"Tom?" Deacon said.

"*Copy,*" Tom said, his voice coming through their earpieces. Tom was another Thomas Security bodyguard, and he was inside the bar as Cami's backup.

"We're coming in to do some surveillance. Where is the client situated?" Deacon asked.

"*Two o'clock from the entry. High table, and Cami is sitting with them. All clear, you should be able to enter and break up easily, since the bar is full,*" Tom said.

"Copy."

James leaned forward to tuck his weapon into the back of his jeans. It was no accident that Mak was at this bar—Thomas Security had arrangements with several bars, and this was one of them. It meant that they could bring weapons in, without questions being asked.

James followed behind Deacon as he walked past the queue and up to the bouncer. He gave the code name 'Vester,' and the bouncer bowed his head slightly, opening the door for them. Inside, they immediately split up. James went to the back of the bar, farther away from Mak, and let Deacon take the post nearest to her. It was another way of trying to stay in the background of this case.

James blended into the crowd, like a lion in long grass. And he was every bit as much a predator.

James couldn't see Deacon, but he didn't need to—they were constantly connected via their earpieces. He could see Mak, though, and his breath halted. She was sitting on a stool, talking to the woman he assumed to be the friend she'd arranged to meet. His eyes traveled down her spine—the deep, backless 'V' of her dress revealing her soft, taut skin. And she wasn't wearing a bra.

"I forgot how cool this bar is," Deacon said. *"We should come here for drinks."*

Deacon obviously wasn't having the same thoughts James was, which was a good thing.

"We don't drink," James said, turning his head as he spoke, hiding his moving lips from anyone who might be watching.

"Yeah. Perhaps in our next life we'll come back as raging party animals," Deacon joked.

In another life they could be and have so many things, including a woman to love. In an attempt to keep his eyes off her almost naked back, James kept an eye on his watch, and the bar patrons, but it was looking to be a boring night at La Casa—just the way he liked it.

"Move to nine o'clock."

Deacon's command captured his full attention. Fast enough to get into position, but slow enough not to cause attention, James moved to nine o'clock.

"Black shirt, Caucasian, green eyes."

"I see him," James said. He stepped to the side, pretending to let someone through, but really he was on autopilot, blending-in mode. He did it so well he barely had to think about it, fortunately because right now his focus was on the man Deacon had identified. The man who was watching Mak. He was good, he did it subtly, but he wasn't good enough.

"I'm running it." Samuel's voice came through his earpiece and James knew Samuel was running the man's face, picked up by one of the hidden cameras on their shirts, through their facial recognition software.

Minutes passed, and the man continued to casually watch her. And Cami. He was with a group of friends, but James knew he'd brought them along as a façade. He was the only one watching her.

"Ooh . . ."

"Samuel," James said, warning him to finish that sentence.

"You're not going to believe this. His name is Adam Avex, a former SAS." SAS was Special Air Services, a Special Forces unit of the British Army. *"But,"* Samuel continued, *"he died. Two years ago."*

"What the fuck?" Deacon swore.

"I've run it twice. I'm not wrong," Samuel said. Samuel was rarely wrong, and certainly not about something like this. He didn't give information like that lightly.

Why was a former SAS guy watching her?

"Cause of death?" James asked.

"Killed in combat."

The earpiece went silent. James imagined Samuel in his office madly running searches, looking for more information. For James and Deacon, they knew what to do: watch, and don't make a move unless he did. They needed as much time as possible to work out what was going on.

Mak covered her mouth as she yawned wide. *She must be*

exhausted, James thought. She'd had a long week in court, not to mention the upheaval they'd created.

He wanted to take her home and tuck her up in bed—after he'd peeled her dress off. *You're not the guy for her*, the voice inside his head reminded him.

James's hand went to his weapon before he had a chance to think about it. His hands were itching to draw it, but he held back. Dead-boy Adam had his hand on Mak's back and was asking if she had a lighter—James could tell by the action he made with his hands—the rolling of his thumb over an imaginary spark-wheel.

James wanted to walk over there, but he had a good idea what Adam was doing, and he wouldn't play into the trap.

"Hold," James instructed his team. He was failing to let Deacon call the shots, but he no longer cared.

Cami stood up, picking up her bag that she'd conveniently hung over the back of Mak's chair, and pretended to search through her bag. She was aware of the entire situation, via her earpiece, and in her faux attempt to find him a lighter he'd had to take a step back, and she'd effectively blocked Mak's body.

Good girl.

Cami put on a good show, throwing a flirty laugh as she came up empty-handed. Adam sat back down, as did Cami, but Adam's eyes were moving like rovers.

"He's assessing her security," James said. He knew the move, because he'd used it a hundred times. Create a scare, not enough to cause a scene, but enough to capture someone's attention. If Cami hadn't been right next to her, Tom would've moved in and revealed himself.

For another forty-five minutes James watched on silently until Adam and his group stood up and left the bar.

Again James and Deacon didn't need to discuss the plan: follow him. The men were standing outside when the Thomas brothers exited and walked casually by them to Deacon's car. James sat in the front passenger seat with his gun in his hand. They were waiting for the cue from Samuel, who would be watching them on CCTV.

"This is bad," Deacon whispered, as if saying the words too loudly would make it all the more real.

"*Go,*" Samuel said, and Deacon pulled out and turned left at the corner.

"*Silver Lexus . . . Fuck, he's in a hurry,*" Samuel said.

"Don't lose him," Deacon said, planting his foot down and speeding through the red traffic light—Samuel was going to have a busy night deleting evidence.

The GPS screen activated as Samuel fed Adam's coordinates to them.

"*Uh . . . he's flying, and this system is too slow. He's moving through the frames too quickly, we might lose him,*" Samuel said, referring to the city's CCTV system.

They were going to have to tail him, and he was definitely going to pick them up—he was no average soldier.

"Go, go, go!" James said, and Deacon did what he did best—drove. The car weaved through the cars on the road and James watched the GPS.

"*You're catching him,*" Samuel said. James could see the two green circles inching together on the screen—Adam was soon going to realize he had a tail.

The wheels screeched as Deacon pulled a hard right, heading west. James lifted his eyes now, but only to squint, searching for Adam's taillights ahead.

Deacon saw them too. "He's going to pick us up any minute," he warned.

"I know. Just follow him," James said.

Deacon kept up the intensity, swinging the ass of the car through the New York City streets—it wasn't called a concrete jungle for nothing. Turn after turn Deacon kept up with him and as hard as Adam tried, he couldn't lose his tail—Deacon was too good.

They followed him for six more blocks before Adam pulled a one-eighty.

"Oh, fuck! Hold on!" Deacon said, not lifting his foot off the accelerator.

Adam was driving straight toward them, and neither car was slowing down.

"He's got his window down!" James said.

Adam swerved at the last minute, firing a round of shots at Deacon's window.

"That motherfucker shot my car!" Deacon was pissed now, and a furious Deacon was a sight to behold.

Deacon pulled the same move, pulling the car in a full one-eighty, chasing down the man who had just damaged his baby. "Bad move, buddy, bad move."

They were hot on Adam's tail now, and Deacon wasn't backing down. They were bumper to bumper, until Deacon nudged Adam's car. The car swerved as Adam fought to keep control of it—a fight he would ultimately lose. The car went up on two wheels and then flipped over as it skidded into the traffic light.

Deacon slammed the car brakes until they came to a stop. He reversed up, and James put the window down, enough to point his weapon into Adam's car. He smelled it as soon as he inhaled.

"Back up, back up!" James said and Deacon changed gears and pressed his foot to the floor as Adam's car ignited into a fiery ball.

"Well, he's definitely dead now," James said, looking at the burning end to their night.

"Get out of there, now," Samuel instructed and the boys obeyed.

12

MAK ASHWOOD

Mak felt like sheets of sandpaper were rubbing her eyes every time she closed them. She'd worked all week and all day. She would devote her life to this case until it was over, until she won. Failure was a possibility in the land of reality, particularly for the third case, the case of Kate Loren. The evidence was weaker, and that worried Mak, but still she refused to accept defeat. She would win, she would do it for the victims, and their loved ones whose hearts were breaking every day.

Yesterday had been a draining day, and she still hadn't recovered. She'd presented more forensic evidence, all the while avoiding the eyes of the victims' families. She could only imagine how hard it must be. It was one thing to know what happened, it was completely another to see it in photographs, and to hear it described in detail. It was brutal, the hardest part of her job. Possibly the hardest thing she'd ever done.

She'd attempted to distract her mind, or numb it at the very least, with a few drinks. She'd met Kayla at a bar downtown and for a few hours she'd managed to suppress her emotions, but as soon as she tucked herself up in bed, they came flooding back. She felt sadness and guilt. She felt like she was hurting the families all over again, but she had to do it, it was part of the process, part of the process that would hopefully provide justice. It wouldn't bring the dead back, but it would make someone pay. If she won.

Mak's phone rang, startling her from her thoughts. She looked at her phone, surprised to see a caller ID associated with a number she had never programmed into her phone.

"James?" Mak said, looking around like she expected him to appear from thin air.

"Hey. How are you?"

"Um . . . fine. How did your number end up in my phone?" Mak sat up on the couch, folding her legs underneath her.

"All of our numbers are programmed in—Cami's, Deacon's, and mine—Samuel did it remotely so we didn't need to access your phone."

"Okay . . . I suppose." Her phone was as boring as her love life, and she couldn't remember the last time she'd sent a raunchy text to someone or anything else potentially embarrassing.

"Anyway, are you busy? I wanted to come over and discuss tracking devices with you. There are a couple of options for you to consider."

"Now?"

"Preferably. I can be there in fifteen minutes," James said.

"Ah, sure . . . I'll see you soon," Mak said.

James said goodbye and ended the call, and then she placed her phone on her lap. Was it weird that James was coming over and not Deacon? Or were they both coming? James hadn't advised either way, but Thomas Security was never forthcoming with details.

Mak sighed and lay back on the couch again, waiting for one or both brothers to arrive. It felt like he was there in five minutes, but it was easy to lose track of time with a muddled mind.

He knocked on the door and as she was sitting up, preparing to answer it, the door swung open wide. He gave her a soft smile, and closed it behind him.

"Hey," he said. "Don't get up."

Mak relaxed back onto the couch and watched as he took one of her dining chairs and placed it about three feet away from the couch. He moved with such grace, something she'd noticed the first time she'd seen him, but each time it seemed to surprise her. He was the perfect combination of lean strength and agility.

"Hi," Mak said, her voice catching in her throat. It kept doing that around him.

"I'm sorry to hijack your night, again, but I want to get this organized," James said.

Mak nodded her head, a non-verbal acceptance of his apology.

"So, I want to put a tracking device on you. It's probably not needed at this stage, but we like to take extra measures . . ." He gave her a lopsided grin that softened his angular features.

"Okay," she said, mustering a smile.

He paused. "Okay? That's your response?"

"Uh . . . What was I supposed to say? Was it a trick question?"

"No, it wasn't a trick question, but you would normally be much more thorough with your questioning. What's wrong?" James asked.

"Well, apparently questioning you and your brother is the only way to get any information. And anyway, I'm not really a 'yes, sir' kind of girl."

His eyes twinkled and they looked browner tonight—not quite so black. "No, you're not, but I like that. Regardless, you're deflecting the question."

Mak debated whether to tell him because she felt weak for feeling the emotions she did. And she hated to be weak. Would he judge her for it? Would he understand? Or would he pity her for being vulnerable? Pity was the worst.

James sat calmly across from her like he had all the time in the world.

"It's just the trial, it's nothing," Mak said.

"It is something, obviously. What in particular are you worried about?"

"I've been presenting evidence all week, and I hate it. It's the worst part of the process. I feel like I'm hurting the families all over again.

They shouldn't have to keep reliving the horror," she said, looking away.

"You're not hurting them. And in a fair and perfect world, they would never have to go through something like that. But that is not the world we live in. You're fighting for their loved ones, you're doing something for them that they can't do for themselves. It's a gift."

"It's a gift if I win," Mak said with a sad smile. "And if I don't, they get nothing."

"Even if you don't win, you gave them a chance—a chance they didn't have before."

"Maybe," Mak said.

A silent moment passed.

"Do you regret taking the case?" James asked.

"No," Mak said. "Maybe I'm a sucker for punishment."

James gave her a beautiful smile—perhaps the first true smile she'd ever seen on his lips. "Well, that makes two of us, then. I think you're very brave to take on such a case. So does the girl at the coffee shop . . ."

"Excuse me?" Mak said, nearly choking on the air that seemed to be getting thicker by the second. That always seemed to happen around him, too.

"I was getting coffee the other day and a news bulletin came up about your case. I'd been away for a few days, so I asked the girl behind the counter what was going on—this was all before Deacon's surprise visit, obviously. She told me she hopes you win, that she's rooting for you. I think a lot of people are. I haven't seen you in court, but Cami told me you're a force to be reckoned with, and she should know.

"Feeling bad for the victims' families makes you human, Mak, nothing else—so don't beat yourself up. It's okay to feel sad about what happened. Lives were brutally ended, and there's nothing nice about that."

He was a good listener, and he was encouraging without telling her things she didn't want to hear. She didn't want him to tell her she would win, she didn't want him to tell her everything was going to be fine. She didn't want a fluffy response, and she liked that he hadn't given it to her.

"Thank you," she said, looking into his eyes. For a pausing second she felt lost in them, but she drew her attention back to the reason for his visit—ignoring her rapidly increasing pulse. "So, what kind of tracking device is this, anyway?"

He sat up straight again, slipping back into his business *persona*. "There's only one option I like, but I'm going to give you two options at this stage, because I want you to have a choice." He reached into his bag and pulled out what looked like a suede jewelry pouch. "This is your first option," he said, handing her the silver bracelet. "Obviously, it's very easy to remove, hence why I don't like it."

Mak put it on her wrist. It looked like a link bracelet you would buy at Tiffany's. "What's the second option?"

He pulled another trick out of his bag, this time holding what looked like a pen box wrapped in the sterile blue fabric used in operating rooms. He didn't open the box but instead tapped it against the palm of his left hand. "This is a bit different, and it's what I have, and what all of our staff has."

He was stalling but Mak was too exhausted to interrogate him. Wearily, she asked, "What is it?"

"It . . . is a very tiny chip, smaller than a pinhead, that we designed in-house at Thomas Security. Due to the frequency it emits, it can't be detected by a regular scanner, and it can't be taken out—at least not very easily."

"Where do you put it?" Mak asked. She leaned forward and held out her palm but he didn't give the box to her.

"That's the thing . . . It needs to be inserted into the abdomen. The chip comes with a loading device. It's like a long needle that is inserted into your side, and then it lodges the chip into your muscle."

"Doesn't that hurt?" Mak instinctively flexed her abdomen.

"That's the problem—it really fucking hurts. I brought some local anesthetic, which I can numb you with, but even that injection will sting like hell. Personally I think it's better just to stick the needle in and get it over with."

"*You're* going to do this? Are you a doctor?"

James grinned. "No, I'm not a doctor, but I've inserted them for almost all of my defense staff without any problems. I'm very good at it." His arrogance was sexy.

"So they just let a guy with no medical training stick needles in them?"

"I said I'm not a doctor, but I didn't say anything about not having medical training. And that's all you need to know," James said. "The choice is yours."

"Is it really a choice?"

"Yes. You will have few choices when we're involved, so you should seize this one. Ultimately, though, I want you safe, and this is the safest option by far. It will hurt going in, but once it's inserted you won't even know it's there. You'll have a thick pin-prick type mark on your skin which will heal like a small cut," he said, shrugging his shoulders.

"Isn't there an in-between option?" Mak asked.

"Yes, there are all kinds of devices. There are some that you can insert just under the skin of your arm, etc. But, if it can be detected it's pointless because they will just cut it out. So, you might as well have the bracelet and save yourself some future pain, if that's the route you take."

Mak scoffed. "Right. And you're positive you're the best person for the job?"

"Positive. Can we do it?" He held her gaze, challenging her, and she hated to back down from a challenge.

"Okay, let's get this over with. What do you want me to do?" Mak was now hyperaware of the compromising position this would put them in. It was hard to be next to him let alone have his hands on her.

He cleared his throat, retrieving items from his bag as he spoke. "Lie down on your left side, facing me. You'll need to slide your top up a little, and the needle will go into the soft flesh between your ribs and your hip bone."

Mak lay down on her side as instructed and bunched her shirt up enough to give him the access he needed.

He snapped latex gloves on his hands, and his chest expanded as he inhaled. "Okay, I'm going to use this little machine to do an ultrasound first. I need to know how deep to insert the needle so that it lodges the tracker into your muscle. You're very small, so I need to make sure I get it right—there isn't as much room for error as with some of my guys."

He placed his hands on her abdomen and Mak flinched. He looked at her, paused for a moment, and then continued. He prodded her skin, presumably feeling for her muscles.

Mak watched him. His eyes were on the small screen he held in one hand, while the other moved a device over her waist.

He was fascinating to watch—his actions quietly confident and assured. He never seemed flustered, never seemed agitated. How was one so calm all of the time?

His neck inched forward, and he squinted at the screen, pressed a button, and then said, "Good."

He put the ultrasound machine back in his bag. "Do you want the anesthetic?"

"No, just hurry up and do it," she said, hoping she wouldn't regret that decision.

He changed gloves, wiped a brown solution over her skin, and then opened a separate blue package and laid a blue drape over her side. He undid the pen-like box.

James looked over his shoulder and then back at her. "Watch the television, don't watch me. It's best you don't look at the needle."

Mak glued her eyes to the television. She wanted to appear brave, but really she was scared shitless.

She jumped again when he put his hand on her side. He pressed his palm down, massaging her waist. "Relax," he said softly.

Mak wanted to tell him that his touch wasn't helping her relax, but she did her best to distract herself and returned her attention to the news. They were showing the footage of the car chase that occurred last night. The footage was static—like something was wrong with the tape—but she'd seen it twice now and could definitely make out two cars: one silver, and one black.

"Did you see this?" Mak asked, watching the replay of the burning car, wondering who had been inside. "*Maniacs...*"

"Ow!" Mak's fingers squeezed the pillow flat and tears sprang up in her eyes.

A strong hand clutched her hip, keeping her still. "Good job," James said. "The needle is in, just one more sting."

Her body was trembling from the pain, and the sting came just a second after his words. But it wasn't a sting. It was a pain that shot through her like a lightning bolt. She groaned, tucking her chin into her neck. Her hair fell over her cheeks, and she was glad it hid her face from him. She couldn't hide her shaking body, though.

"All done, I promise," he said, with one hand still gripping her hip.

She heard him rustling around for something as she gasped for breath. The needle seemed to have sucked the air out of her lungs as he withdrew it. Something wet and soft wiped over the insertion point, and then she felt him place a bandage on her skin. His rubber gloves came off, and then with a bare hand, he pressed down on the bandage. Mak wasn't sure if it physically helped ease the pain, or if it was just in her mind, but either way it felt good—so good.

He surprised her when he swept the hair off her cheek, tucking it behind her ear. His eyes, normally a wall to his thoughts, seemed more transparent now. Pride? Lust? Or was she just delusional with pain?

"The pain should start to settle down now." There was no hardness in his voice. "You have a high pain threshold."

She raised her eyebrows in doubt.

"I've had grown men four times your size howling as I inserted their trackers. I should show the film of your insertion to my men next time they bitch and complain."

She smiled. She wondered if he was just being kind, but he seemed genuine enough. A thought occurred to her, one that would've been helpful five minutes ago. "I realize it's a bit late for this ... but you never told me how you get the tracker out."

He bit his lip. "It's best you don't. When you no longer need it,

Samuel will turn it off remotely. It won't emit radiation so it's safe to leave inside of you. People have metal screws and silicone implants and all kinds of things inserted into their body. This is no different, and it won't cause you any problems."

Mak felt her body relaxing, and she felt well enough that she *could* sit up again, but he still had his hand on her waist and she didn't want him to let go. She stayed where she was.

"So, who inserted your tracker if you do all of the insertions?"

The question earned her another true smile. "I did it myself. I was the first one—the guinea pig, as such." He paused, seeming to reflect on his words. "I'm always the guinea pig—I wouldn't ask someone to do something I wouldn't. Not to mention it's better to test it on my body. If it goes badly, at least I don't have to worry about staff suing me."

Mak laughed softly. "Very true."

He looked back at the insertion site then lifted his hand. She missed the heat of his touch immediately.

"How are you feeling?" James asked.

"Good," Mak said, pushing herself upright. He steadied her, and once he seemed confident she wasn't going to faint, he let her go, and began packing everything back into his bag.

"Well, this has been a fun Saturday night for you," Mak joked.

"Actually, this has been a pretty good Saturday night," he said.

"Why? Because you like inflicting pain on others?"

His chest shook as he laughed. "Sometimes, Mak, sometimes. But that's not what I meant."

"What did you mean, then?" She was back at her prime, ready to interrogate him.

"I meant," he said, zipping up his bag, "exactly what I said. My life is not very fun, Mak. On a Saturday night I'm usually either working, or I'm asleep. I live a lifestyle that is not conducive to a social life."

"You must have some social life," Mak said.

"No, I really don't. I'm always on stand-by for my company, even when I'm not technically working. So that means no vacations, no nights out on the town, no parties at friend's houses."

"You went to Zahra and Jayce's engagement party," Mak said, ignoring the throbbing pain that had started up in her side.

"I went to say hello, and because my company was overseeing the security, I wanted to check in. I wasn't drinking, and I didn't stay long. What you saw was the extent of my social life . . . Not very exciting, is it?" he asked, relaxing back into the chair.

"No, not really," Mak said, turning his words over, strategizing how to continue to press him on this matter.

"When do you see your family, then?"

"That's a very difficult task, and I haven't seen them for a long time," James said. "I don't have a girlfriend, either, if that was going to be your next question. Neither Deacon nor I do . . . It's best to avoid relationships, given our field of work."

Hmm. It was good to know he didn't have a girlfriend but simultaneously he'd made it very clear he didn't want one, either. As they sat across from each other, Mak thought they were both playing the same game—trying to read each other's thoughts.

"Do all your employees adopt this mentality, or is it just you and your brother?"

"Cami is of the same opinion. The others have different roles in the company, so they can do as they please," James said.

"Is Cami a partner at Thomas Security?"

"She's a partner, of sorts."

Mak rolled her eyes. "I like her," she said.

"Good," James said. "If you didn't get along it would be a bit of a problem, considering how much time you're going to spend together."

He seemed in a talkative mood, and in no hurry to leave, so she pressed on. "Are you ever anyone's bodyguard?" Mak asked.

"Sometimes when we take on a new client I might act as a bodyguard in the interim, but it's better if I'm in the office planning and overseeing the security strategies. I can't do that if I'm with a client all day."

"What is your background?"

"Nice try. I can't tell you that, Mak. It's classified."

"Classified is a very vague term—it could mean anything."

"Take it to mean whatever you want it to mean." He crossed his arms over his chest—the conversation was apparently over.

Mak crossed her arms over her chest, mirroring his closed-off body language.

He smirked. They were at a stalemate, and the air crackled between them.

James didn't back down; he seemed to enjoy it—Mak wasn't the only one who liked a challenge.

"Is Deacon's background also classified?"

He shook his head slowly. "You'll have to ask him that."

"And Cami's?"

"Ask her tomorrow," he said.

"Are you going to tell me anything else?"

"No. I've said far too much already." His mood seemed to change as he said the words and the playfulness dropped out of his eyes like a falling star. He pulled his phone from his pocket. "I need to check if your tracker is working before I leave," he said, holding the phone up to his ear.

"Samuel, all good? . . . Okay, thanks. I'll see you soon," he said and then hung up and slid his phone back into his pocket.

"It's working perfectly," he said to Mak. "I should go." He stood up, slinging his bag over his shoulder. She wondered how much Thomas Security spent on equipment—it would have to be something astronomical.

Mak walked him to the door.

"Good night, Mak," he said as he left, closing the door behind him.

He didn't pause, he didn't linger, but she didn't miss the deepness of his voice.

13

JAMES THOMAS

His feet bounced off the road, expending the energy in his body. The streets of New York were quieter this morning, and he was grateful for the solitude as he ran over the Brooklyn Bridge.

All night, and it had been a long night, he'd thought of her. The tracker was probably unnecessary at this stage; even Samuel, who erred on the cautious side, questioned it. But they didn't know what they were dealing with, and until they did, and could aptly create a suitable security plan for her, James wanted to take every precaution possible.

But Deacon was going to have a fit when he woke up. A massive, verbal-inducing fit. Deacon could've inserted the tracker, but James had done five times as many insertions as he had, and he wanted her to have the best. He had also wanted to be alone with her. He had wanted a few minutes to talk to her, and to try and understand his feelings for her. This was new territory for him, and he was struggling with it. Paris had awoken a sense of longing that he'd never known before. It wasn't that he wanted a family, but in that moment, when he'd tried to save Angela, he'd seen a glimpse of what life could be like with a partner—with someone to love. And to be loved in return.

James closed his eyes for a moment as he continued to run. He was torturing himself, but he didn't know how to stop it.

He'd taken his time with the insertion. He didn't want to make a mistake, but he'd also been in no hurry to get the job done. It was a battle not to be distracted by the reaction he felt to touching her. He enjoyed being with her, he enjoyed talking to her, and they were so compatible. And he was sure now that the attraction was mutual. But, reality had come crashing back down when she reminded him of the one thing he wanted to forget: his past.

James slowed to a walk and then took a break, leaning against the bridge railing, looking at the water below.

He'd also spent a lot of last night thinking about the events that led up to Nicole's death and where things went so wrong—what had ultimately led to her and Deacon being captured. James knew they could avoid making the same mistakes now—they were better equipped with more experience. They had become very good at protecting people, very good. Not to mention James had a different skillset than Deacon. But that still didn't guarantee James could protect Mak. There were factors he couldn't control, and there was a lot more risk associated with his past. And while Thomas Security never took risks with their clients, James couldn't say the same thing for himself personally. He did take occasional risks—they were measured risks, but risks nonetheless. And a risk could always land someone in the clutches of harm—especially a girlfriend.

James looked at his watch: it was seven in the morning. He wanted to speak to her. He did legitimately need to call her—to confirm her wound wasn't bleeding—but that was a call his brother could make. He dialed her number anyway, and it rang seven times before she picked up.

"Hey," she said with a sweet, sleepy voice.

She didn't say anything else, and he knew she was barely awake— if she was, she probably wouldn't have answered with such a wanton voice.

And that presented the second problem. Even if he could protect her, there was an aspect he couldn't control. Could she fall in love with a man with a secret past, a past she knew nothing about? And if by some miracle she did, could she still love him if one day he told her the truth? Or would she come to hate him?

"James?" Mak said, sounding almost alarmed now. There wasn't a trace of huskiness left in her voice.

"Hi. Sorry, I got distracted. I woke you, didn't I?"

"Yes, actually, you did. I hope it was for a good reason," she said with a tone of humor. She sounded more like herself this morning.

"It's not, *actually*." He found himself smiling—something he'd done more of with her in the past week than he'd done in the past ten years. "I just wanted to check on your insertion wound. Take a look at it, is it bleeding?"

Sometimes the wounds did leak a little, but he doubted hers would; her blood had clotted fast. And he hadn't been lying about her pain threshold. It was high, and that was good if she were ever kidnapped—she'd be able to hold out longer and give him more time to get to her. It was a horrible thought, but it was a thought that pleased him.

He heard a ruffling noise, which he assumed were her sheets.

"The bandage looks fine. Should I take it off and look underneath?"

"You can leave it on for a little while longer, but take it off this afternoon. If it's not bleeding through the bandage, though, I'm not concerned," James said.

"Okay," Mak replied. "Why are you up so early? Don't you know Sundays are for sleeping in?"

James chuckled. He didn't sleep in, not even on Sundays. He would like to sleep in, though—if he were in her bed. "No. I'm running. Well, I was running. I just took a quick break and thought I'd check in. So if you're not bleeding to death, I'll let you get back to sleep."

She scoffed. "I'm wide awake now, so sleep is probably out of the question. I might as well call my sister and wake her up for an early brunch. What are you doing today?"

"Working," James said. He was always working. "Mak . . . if you ever need anything, call me first, on this number, okay?"

"Sure," she said, sounding taken aback, which was a fair reaction but he wanted her to know she could call him, if she needed to, or wanted to—any time of the day or night.

"Have a good day, Mak," he said.

"I will. You, too. Bye."

He zipped his phone back into his shorts pocket and began the run home. He'd only taken a few measly steps before his phone rang: *Deacon.*

"Hello," James said politely. He wasn't prepared to get into a heated discussion over the phone.

"Hi. We've got breakfast waiting for you in Samuel's office," Deacon said. It was his polite way of calling a family meeting.

"I'm on the bridge, so I'll be there soon," James said, beginning the run home for the second time.

James arrived sweaty and hungry. He didn't bother to shower, but went straight up to Samuel's office. *Best to get this over with.*

When he walked into Samuel's office, their little family was gathered around a spread of baked goods and coffee. They didn't do brunch, but he supposed this was their version of it. James picked up a croissant, indulging in the high-calorie delight. He washed it down with a bottle of water, and then his coffee. And then he was ready to talk.

"I could've inserted the tracker," Deacon said with an edge of hostility.

"I know that, but I wanted to do it," James said. "Look, I know you're concerned, and I know this is more about Nicole than it is about Mak, but I didn't go there last night to hit on her. I have more experience inserting the trackers, and you know it, and I wanted to talk to her . . ."

"Talk to her about what?" Deacon asked.

"To get to know her a little better."

"If you're not planning to pursue her, why do you want to get to know her? You don't do that with other clients, do you?" Deacon raised one eyebrow. "I know what you're thinking. You're trying to figure out if there's some way you can make this happen. Let me tell you, there isn't. And if the memory of Nicole's mutilated body isn't enough to deter you, then I don't know what would be. So have it your way, pursue her, but just remember if her blood ends up on your hands, you'll have no one to blame but yourself, and you will experience a kind of heartache you never thought possible."

James didn't respond, because some part of him still thought there was a good chance they could protect her. He'd protected presidents in war zones, he'd transported and protected high-profile prisoners, and he'd protected the cartel and gang members with more enemies than he had. And they'd protected all of their clients without a death incident—excluding Kyoji Tohmatsu. But there was no guarantee, and that was the problem.

"How did she do with the tracker?" Cami asked.

"Good," James said proudly. "Better than you."

He ducked in anticipation, just missing the sachet of sugar that came hurtling at him.

"Liar! I only swore once!"

James wiggled his eyebrows. "Once too many."

"That little shit," Cami said.

"You want to know something really funny?" James asked Deacon. "I'd just finished the ultrasound so I told her to watch the television so she didn't see the needle. Anyway, I couldn't believe it— a bulletin came on showing our car chase the night before. She asked me if I'd seen the footage, and then in the most disapproving tone, she said 'maniacs'."

Deacon cracked the faintest hint of a smile.

Cami asked, "What did you say to her?"

James scoffed. "Nothing. I jabbed the needle in, and she forgot all about the car chase."

Deacon's smile grew a little more, and James knew in a few hours he'd laugh at that comment.

James took a fruit salad from the table—he was not nearly done with breakfast.

"Samuel, what ended up happening with the police about that car chase?" James asked.

Samuel took a tiny sip of his coffee. He always drank it like that, and James thought it must get cold before he got to the bottom of the cup. "It's been handled. That little experience cost you quite a bit of dough, though, not to mention Deacon's car."

The dough was in bribe money—hush money—and Deacon's car needed major repairs. "That's unfortunate," James said, but he didn't regret it. He would have preferred Adam alive, though—at least then he could've extracted some information.

"I want my car fixed," Deacon said with the patience of a four-year-old.

Thomas Security had an ample fleet of identical cars, so it wasn't like Deacon was making a huge sacrifice by driving another car, but he had become very attached to his vehicle.

"I've got some news about Adam," Samuel said, ignoring Deacon. "I'm grasping at straws here, because it could be an error—phone tower data is not always correct, and someone could've stolen his phone—but, two days post death—at least the date recorded in his military records—his phone connected to a tower in Italy, in the Melfi region. One connection, and then he disappeared again. So far I haven't been able to find a trace of him, or an alias to link him to. He's Special Forces, though, so it's not surprising he knew how to disappear."

Adam was a smart guy—otherwise he'd never have made it into SAS—so he knew not to turn his phone on, or even connect the battery. If he did, something had gone wrong in his plan, and he was desperate. Or it wasn't him at all.

But if Adam had made it to Italy, and he was watching Mak now, there was a good chance he'd made friends with the Camarro boys at some stage, and they'd sent him to New York. James was confident they were behind the notes, and that they had used Adam Avex as a postman.

James's phone vibrated on the table: *Jayce Tohmatsu.*

Their last exchange had been shortly after Jayce had found out they hadn't taken on Mak Ashwood. Jayce had a hard time with the word 'no' and he hadn't been happy with their decision.

"Jayce," James said in his customary greeting.

"Hey. Have you got a minute?"

"Sure," James said, stretching his legs out under the table.

"Okay. I was planning to work from home today, so I gave Lenny the day off—it's his daughter's birthday. But something's come up, and I want to go to the Hamptons for the day. Do you have someone to cover him? I don't want to be an asshole and tell him he's got to work, but I really need to have a look at this site, and I can only do it today."

Lenny was Jayce's bodyguard, and he was one of their best men. He was that beautiful mix of hard and soft—he was a killer at the office, and a family man at home.

"Hang on," James said, and then put the call on mute. "Deacon, Jayce needs someone for the day because Lenny's off. I'll go with him, but you're around if Cami needs you, right?"

Deacon rolled his eyes but nodded his head. Mak had a body-guard, and now a team of nine ghosts. Ghosts were the guys who lived in the shadows. They watched everything that went on around the client. They looked for watching eyes, for snipers, for people who looked anxious—anything that seemed abnormal.

"Jayce, I'll go with you. What time do you want to leave?" James said, standing up.

"Now," Jayce said, laughing. When he decided on something, that was it—he had to have it, and he had to have it right then.

"I'll be at your apartment in thirty minutes."

"Thanks, I appreciate it," Jayce said, and then hung up without a goodbye.

"I'll probably be gone most of the day, so call me if anything comes up," James said, looking at each of them, but lingering on Cami a little longer.

"Yes, yes. Have fun," she said, waving him away.

James knocked on the door to Jayce and Zahra's apartment, despite having the code to let himself in. He'd designed the security for the entire building, and had his own access code, just in case. Samuel could always unlock the doors for him, but even that took a few seconds, and sometimes a few seconds was one second too many.

Zahra opened the door, her eyes sparkling like emerald gems. The first time James had seen her he was sure they were contact lenses but they weren't.

"He's on the phone, as usual." She tilted her head to the side and pressed her lips together before she let out a small laugh.

Jayce was a complete workaholic, and he was very lucky he'd found an independent woman who didn't care that his work consumed his life.

"Of course," James said, rolling his eyes. "Wow, this place is looking great." It was an awesome apartment. James had seen it before Jayce had surprised Zahra with it. It looked the same now, but it felt like a home; it was infused with their personal touches. Being the lead interior designer for his firm, it was only natural she would design the apartment, except she'd thought she was doing it for a client.

James looked over the photos and instantly knew they had come from Thomas Security's surveillance. "How did you get these?"

"There was a note in the photo album you gave us for our engagement, advising to email if we wanted any enlargements. I can see you were highly involved in that," she said, poking his shoulder.

"I put my foot in it." James laughed. "Cami organized that for you. I honestly had no idea until she put it in my arms to take with me."

"We sent a thank you note, but please thank her personally for us. There were some nice moments in among all of that," she said quietly, her eyes looking at the photograph of her and Jayce.

"There always are," James said. In the midst of a security scare, particularly one like they had, it's hard to see the good, the blessings of life. It's easier from the outside, for the people like James who were watching them, but all the clients see is fear and pain.

"Hey," Jayce said, walking toward him with his hand outstretched. "Thanks for this, especially at such short notice."

"No problem. Are you ready?"

Jayce retrieved his briefcase from the dining table and wrapped Zahra up in his arms. "I'll be back in time for family dinner," he said before kissing her goodbye.

"Drive safe," she said, closing the door behind them.

The elevator doors opened and Jayce punched in a code, which prevented the elevator from stopping at any other floor, taking them directly to the basement parking level—another security measure.

"So, what are we doing in the Hamptons?" James asked. He'd been to the Hamptons only once before, and he couldn't say he was a fan.

James surveyed the parking lot before he led Jayce to his car. When they were both inside, James started the engine and reversed out of the parking bay.

"I got a call last night about a development site. It's not on the market but apparently the owner has said he might be willing to sell. I'd be looking to put four homes on the site."

"How many projects do you have going on at the moment?" James said, keeping his eyes on the traffic.

"Too many. But you know me, I don't like to let a good opportunity pass me by," he said, checking something on his phone. "Get this, though. If I do it, I'll be doing it via Kyoji's estate. Can you imagine the look on his face if he found out he was buying property in the Hamptons?"

James laughed. Kyoji—the ultimate bad-boy gangster—would not fit in in the Hamptons. His investments had tended toward seedy nightclubs and strip clubs.

"As long as he didn't have to live there he would have been okay with it," James said. Kyoji might have played by a different set of rules, but he was as savvy a businessman as Jayce.

"So, what's new with you? I was very pleased to hear that Mak Ashwood is now under Thomas Security," Jayce said.

"Yes, she is. Things change all the time, but she'll stay with us for the time being," James said, giving an evasive answer.

"What changed your mind?"

"I can't discuss our clients with you—you know that," James said.

"She's an interesting woman. She's beautiful; she looks dainty almost, don't you think? Like you could bump her and she'd fall over. But then she walks into the courtroom and is ripping these mob guys apart. I think it's fucking brilliant," Jayce said.

"I think most agree with you," James said.

Jayce smirked. "And what do you think?"

"I think she's a client, and I'm not discussing her," James said, not playing Jayce's game.

"Oh come on, you're a guy, so don't tell me you don't agree. Not to mention, I saw how you looked at her at my engagement party. You weren't expecting her to be there—I think it's the one time I've ever seen you slip up."

"You're reaching, Jayce," James said.

"Whatever," he said. "What do you think about her husband's disappearance?"

"Missing persons are unfortunately not uncommon," James said.

"Mmm. He seemed to be a smart guy. Ambitious, too. Real estate developments in foreign countries are high-risk, especially for a twenty-two-year-old guy. Even I didn't do that until I was . . . twenty-five, I think."

What? James' fingers tingled on the steering wheel. Her husband had designed and licensed a software program for real estate developers—he was not a developer. This information had to have come through Maya, or Mak directly. It wasn't public knowledge otherwise they'd know about it. *Why would he need to lie about his job?*

"He did seem to be," James said, lowering his foot slightly on the accelerator. He wanted to get to the Hamptons as soon as possible and get Jayce out of the car so he could make a call.

14

MAK ASHWOOD

"Do you need anything before I leave?" Cami asked, standing in Mak's living room. Her legs were concealed behind a box that Mak still hadn't unpacked.

"No, thank you. I'm staying in for the rest of the night. I want to shower and do a review before court tomorrow. Can you be here at six? I need to talk with my team before the trial resumes."

"Sure, I can be here any time you need me. If you want to leave earlier, just send me a message—it doesn't matter if it's in the middle of the night."

"Thanks, Cami. Six will be fine," Mak said, moving toward the door. They had been out most of the day. It had started with brunch, and then a few errands, finishing with her late Sunday afternoon barre class—it was the only one she could regularly commit to, and her mental clarity depended on it.

Mak had felt better after James Thomas's visit. She didn't know if it was the distraction he provided, or just talking about the trial, but now the unwanted emotions were creeping back in. And tomorrow would be another big day in the courtroom.

She closed the door behind Cami and breathed a sigh of relief.

Mak liked to be alone when she was in one of these moods—she didn't like people to see her weaknesses.

She went straight into her bathroom and turned on the shower. She liked it warm, but not hot—comfortable enough to withstand the twenty-minute shower that was her everyday luxury.

When her hair was washed, legs shaved, body exfoliated and face washed, she stepped out of the shower. The bathroom was misty and the constant heat had gradually built to create a fog that blurred her reflection in the mirror. She dried herself and then lathered her body, head to toe, in moisturizer.

You're helping them. You're giving them a chance. You're not hurting them.

They were the words on repeat in her mind as she fought for the courage she would need in court tomorrow.

You can do this.

She dressed in a clean set of pajamas and then picked up her handbag and briefcase, and dumped them all onto her bed. She climbed under the sheets, propping her back up with pillows. Mak dragged her handbag closer to her, searching for the old-school paper diary she still used. Her hand fumbled in the oversized carry-all until her fingers hit something unfamiliar.

She froze.

No. She pulled out a white scroll.

How?

She stared at it like it had been sent from Mars. And then she slipped the ribbon off.

Contact. Wait out.

Mak's heart ran wild, leaping and hurdling as she read the note over and over again. It made no sense to her. She bit down on her thumb, thinking over her day. Cami had been with her every minute —she'd sat beside her at brunch and had walked beside her. She hadn't been alone at all. Cami had even accompanied her to the bathroom, and someone certainly didn't slip it into her bag while it was hanging in the stall.

Her crossed legs began to bounce, a reaction of the fear dominating her body. She had to call security, and she should call Cami, but there was only one person she wanted to speak to now.

James answered on the second ring. "Mak?"

She didn't answer, her words caught in her throat.

"What's wrong?" James asked.

"I don't know . . . I found another scroll note. It was in my handbag. It must have been slipped in there sometime today," Mak said, hugging her knees to her chest.

"What?" James sounded very unimpressed, and Mak hoped Cami wasn't going to get in trouble for this. "What does it say?"

Mak repeated the words on the scroll. "The note doesn't make sense at all. I mean, the others didn't either, but this one really doesn't."

"It's not supposed to, it's not for you. What room are you in? Are the curtains drawn?"

Mak heard the sound of a car starting.

"I'm in my bedroom," she said, then looked at the curtains. "Yes, they're drawn."

"Good. Stay on the phone with me, but go into your bathroom and lock the door. Now," he said.

"James, what does it mean?"

"Are you in the bathroom?"

"I'm going," Mak said, climbing out of her bed.

"Lock the door. Is it locked?"

"Yes, it's locked. Tell me what's going on!"

"I will when I get there, which will be in a few minutes. I'm coming up with Deacon. Do not unlock the door for anyone other than us, including our security. Understood?"

"Yes, but what the hell is going on?"

"Stay on the phone, Mak. Don't hang up. Think about today—when did you leave your bag unattended?"

"I didn't, and Cami was with me all day. She literally did not leave my side," Mak said, closing the toilet lid and sitting on it. Her bathroom suddenly felt very small and the mirrors were still misted, which did nothing to ease her panic.

"What did you do? Talk me through your day," James said.

"Um . . . I went to brunch and—"

"Where was your handbag while you were eating?"

"I put it underneath the table, by my feet. The restaurant was packed, so there was no room to hang it on my chair."

"Okay, where to after brunch?"

"We walked to a few places, errands I had to run. My bag was hung over my shoulder, and I didn't put it down at all. And then I went to my barre class before we came home," Mak said, completing the summary.

"Your regular barre class?"

"Yes. But Cami was there, and our bags were in the room with us."

"It doesn't matter—routine presents an opportunity because it makes you predictable."

"But I know most of those girls," Mak said, unable to imagine any of them putting a note into her bag.

"You don't know them, you only think you do. People can be persuaded very easily," James said. "Open the bathroom door."

Already? Mak hesitated, remembering she was in her pajamas, without a bra.

She put her arms over her chest and unlocked the door. James greeted her with a onceover but he didn't laugh, or make a comment; in fact, his face was completely unreadable.

"Are you okay?" James asked.

"Not really, you're freaking me out," Mak said, rubbing her arms that were chilled with fright.

"I'm not trying to. Come out of the bathroom," he said, stepping to the side to give her room to walk past.

"Can you please tell me what that note means?" Mak said, standing beside her bed.

James looked like he wasn't going to tell her, but he did. "It's a military phrase. It's the first thing you say when you've been engaged by the enemy. The note was intended for us, not you. Someone is watching you, and they know you have protection. It's a warning."

"A warning for what?" Mak said, sitting down on the edge of her bed, taking the weight off her shaky legs.

"I don't know yet," James said distractedly. He looked over his shoulder, and Mak peered behind him to see Deacon Thomas walking toward them. He nodded at James, a silent communication of sorts—a conversation that Mak knew she was deliberately being left out of.

"Hey, Mak," Deacon said.

"Can you please pack a bag?" James continued. "We need to move you out of here tonight."

"What? No! It's the middle of the night, and I need to get a few hours of sleep before court tomorrow."

"Mak, I can't guarantee you're safe here. It's not my apartment of choice for you, so it's best if you stay in the vacant apartment at Thomas Security until we can source a better place for you," he said calmly.

"Move again? No. I'm in the middle of the biggest trial of my life, and I've already moved once. Can't you just increase the security here?" Mak was standing up again, the frustration giving her body a new lease on life.

"It's not the ideal apartment—"

"And whose fault is that? You were the one who said Thomas Security couldn't take me on and then proceeded to set me up with a company that you then decided you didn't like. If you had just done this from the start, we might not be in this situation."

"I know, I made a mistake," James said, looking directly at her.

"*We* made a mistake, Mak," Deacon chipped in. "We realize this is far from ideal, but keeping you safe comes before convenience. And the sooner we get going, the sooner you can go to bed. We're not trying to make this difficult, but staying here is really not a good idea."

Mak rubbed her gritty eyes. "I can't believe this is happening tonight of all nights."

"I think it's intentional that it happened tonight of all nights," James said. "I don't believe in coincidence. They're trying to rattle you before what is going to be a big day tomorrow, right?"

He was right, and that fact made Mak's ears steam with anger. And moving and sleeping somewhere foreign was only going to make it worse.

"Right," Mak said, almost spitting out the word. "Do I have a choice about moving tonight?"

"You have a choice about doing it the easy way or the hard way," James said, his carefree appearance not faltering. It infuriated her further. She was angry about the note, angry that she was letting them upset her, and she was anxious about tomorrow. It was a bad combination.

"What kind of a choice is that?" Mak asked, glaring at him.

"You're wasting time," he said softly. Mak didn't want soft, she wanted him to be angry—to feel as pissed off as she did.

"Why are you so calm? It's irritating!" Mak said.

Deacon cracked a wide smile. "I'm *so* glad someone's finally said that to him," he said, chuckling as he patted his brother on the shoulder and then walked out of the room.

James remained leaning against the doorframe like they were discussing the weather. "Pack for a couple days, and we'll go from there," he said.

Mak puffed out a frustrated sigh. She didn't want to waste any more time, but she felt like by moving in the middle of the night, it was letting whoever sent her that message win. They wanted to cause upheaval in her life, and they'd succeeded.

"Can you please leave so I can change?" Mak threw in "please" in order not to sound like a complete bitch, especially considering she'd just told him he was irritating. The calmness really was fury-provoking, though.

"You've got five minutes, and I'm coming back in," he said and then closed the door behind him.

Mak quickly changed into a pair of jeans and a sweater, and then pulled out three suits for court and layered them into one suit bag. She dashed into the bathroom and packed three bags of makeup and toiletries. She then threw some underwear, pajamas, shoes, and other necessities onto the bed. And then ran into a hurdle: she had no idea which box her overnight bag was packed in.

She was madly pulling things out of the three unpacked boxes she had in her room when James walked back in, and he looked a little shocked. "What are you doing?"

She looked around her, realizing that it looked like she'd just ransacked her own bedroom. "I can't find my overnight bag. I don't know which box it's in," Mak said, depositing even more belongings on the floor.

James came to her. "Stop, stop. You don't need an overnight bag." He put his hand on her forearm, gently guiding her away from the box. He looked at the bed. "Is this everything you're packing tonight?"

Mak nodded her head, noticing her lacy lingerie was in full view.

James reached for one of her pillows and removed the pillowcase. He handed it to her. "Put the loose things in here and I'll carry the cosmetic bags and suit bag. Let's go." He picked up the three bags, cradling them in one arm, and then picked up the suit bag with the other.

"Oh, I need all those files too," Mak said, quickly packing her things into the pillowcase.

"Deacon!" James yelled, and Deacon materialized in her bedroom. "Can you please take Mak's notes?"

"Of course," he said. "Do they all go together in here, Mak?" Deacon asked, holding open the bag.

"Yeah, that's fine, I'll sort them out when we get to the apartment. Thanks."

Mak's eyes traveled over her bedroom, wondering if she'd forgotten anything. James seemed to be able to read her mind.

"If you need anything else, let me know, and I'll come back and get it. Even if it's in the middle of the night, that'll be fine. Let's go," he said for the second time.

Mak followed James, and Deacon followed behind her. And this order resumed once they got out of the elevator and moved toward the waiting car.

"You need to sit in the back," James said, before climbing into the passenger seat and Deacon into the driver's seat.

The car was deadly silent on the drive to Thomas Security. No one spoke, no radio played, no phones rang. Mak was equally relieved and surprised when they pulled into the parking lot. Every single car was the same: a black sedan. They looked like soldiers lined up in perfect organization. And there must have been at least thirty in the lot. Mak wondered how many more there were during the day.

The men carried all of her belongings into the elevator and when Mak could no longer bear the silence, she spoke. "Why do you have a spare apartment here? How many apartments are there?"

"We keep one apartment vacant for purposes just like this. Our clients need it from time to time. It's fully stocked like a hotel room, including tea, coffee, and juice. Anything else you need, just let me know," James said.

"And how many apartments are there?" Mak asked, not giving him a chance to ignore her question.

"There are five, Mak," he said finally.

The elevator sang a high-pitched note, and they stepped out. James entered a code, opening the apartment door.

Mak's eyes bounced over the apartment—it was very nice, nicer than the apartment she had been living in prior to this entire ordeal.

They put her belongings in what she assumed to be the bedroom and then they were back in front of her.

"There is a phone by the bed; our numbers are programmed into it. Alternatively, call my cell if you need anything," James said.

Mak noticed that he always instructed her to contact him first. Mak was of the understanding that the brothers ran the company together, but James certainly seemed to be the one in charge.

"Okay," Mak said with a hint of resignation. She wasn't pleased about being here, but she was pleased that she was safe.

The brothers left and Mak went into the bedroom. She changed back into her pajamas, brushed her teeth, again, and pulled out some notes. It was past one in the morning, and she had to be up at five, but she knew she'd have a better chance of sleeping if her mind was prepared.

When she was confident in her preparations, she turned off the light and pulled the blankets up under her chin, but her eyes refused to close.

Contact. Wait out.

What were they waiting for? And how long would they have to wait?

15

JAMES THOMAS

The black sheet of sky was littered with twinkling stars. James lay on the rooftop lounge chair, staring at the cosmos above him. Nature had always been his refuge, probably due to the amount of time he'd spent outdoors during his training years and on various missions. No matter the magnitude of his problems, nature had a good way of bringing it back into perspective. He was but one small soul in this world, a world that would go on long after he passed.

The rooftop door opened, and James rolled his head to the side. Deacon walked toward him.

"Do you want to be alone?" Deacon asked, standing at the foot of the second chair.

"No, it's fine, sit down," James said, swinging his legs down and sitting up to face Deacon. "I'm not going to do it. I'm not going to pursue her."

"It's the right decision, James," Deacon said.

"I'd almost convinced myself that I could do it . . . that between you, Samuel, Cami, and me, we could cover every base and protect her. And then that note slipped through and it was the perfect reminder that I can't always control every factor," James said, sighing. "I'm in no hurry to move her out of here, though. I'll find her an apartment tomorrow, but I don't want her to leave Thomas Security until her trial is over." They normally tried to have clients out of Thomas Security within a week, in the event another client needed the apartment, but James was prepared to risk it because right now she was his priority.

"It's going to be harder for you to resist her, knowing she's sleeping one floor down," Deacon said.

James already knew that, but protecting her came first. "I don't care, I'll deal with it. I want her to be safe, and nowhere is safer than this building."

Deacon nodded his head in agreement. "You have thought about what is going to happen if she wins, though, right?"

James grimaced. "That they might go from trying to scare her to teaching her a lesson?"

"Exactly," Deacon said, biting his lip.

"I know. Part of me doesn't want her to win for that reason, but if she doesn't win, she will beat herself up for a long time over this case, and I don't want her to go through that either," James said, looking at his hands.

"We'll just have to see how it goes. What else can we do at this stage?"

Deacon was right, there was nothing to do but wait it out.

"At least she's entertaining," Deacon said with a hint of a smile. *"How are you so calm? It's irritating!"* he said, impersonating Mak. "That was fucking hilarious! You should've seen Samuel giggling a few minutes ago in his office. He said he's going to save that camera footage somewhere very safe."

James chuckled—even he'd thought it was funny.

Deacon rubbed his neck like he had a crick in it, and James thought it was probably due to the emotional stress he'd been causing him.

"You're right that something has changed since Paris. If I'd met Mak before that happened, the attraction would've been there, of course, but I would never have allowed myself to even consider the possibility of a relationship. I was given something I had never wanted, or even considered, and now I can't stop thinking about how lonely our lives are. I find myself wishing, hoping, that the future can be different but it can't—our pasts have made sure of that," James mused, more to himself than Deacon.

Deacon nodded slowly, thoughtfully.

"We need to keep a very close eye on her," James said, getting back on track. "I want to follow her tomorrow, but I don't want her to know I'm there. You need to be in that courtroom with a hidden camera, and I'll be outside. We have to be there as backup for Cami in case something happens."

"I agree," Deacon said confidently.

James looked at his watch. It was two in the morning but he didn't feel tired at all. And he didn't want to lie in bed, tormenting his mind. He'd made the decision not to pursue her, and now he had to accept it.

"You're not going to sleep tonight, are you?" Deacon asked.

"I thought I might go to the gym and release some of this frustration."

"Up for a bit of boxing? I'll hold the pads since I've been such a pain in the ass lately." It was Deacon's version of an apology.

James smiled; it was exactly what he needed. He wanted to beat the shit out of something, or someone, and if Deacon had offered himself up, that was his problem. "Let's go, brother."

James watched the live camera footage as Mak stood before the jury. "These are photographs of the injuries sustained by Ms. Nelson. Eleven broken ribs, right and left arm fractures, a broken jaw, collarbone fractures, rib and pelvic fractures, ligature marks on her throat and fractured cartilage in her neck, a deep laceration on her thigh, bruising and laceration of her cervix, bruising of her abdomen, and finally, a ruptured spleen." Mak unhurriedly shuffled the evidence photographs through her hands, one by one as she stated the injuries, and then handed them to the juror in front of her.

She turned back to the man under oath. She leaned one arm against the juror stand, and rested the other on her hip. She appeared to hold the man's gaze. "You barely left an inch of her untouched, didn't you?"

"Objection!"

"Does it make you feel powerful to beat a woman beyond recognition—?"

Mak's voice was strong and confident, the disgust as clear as the blue sky, and she didn't give any indication that she was nervous or worried about the trial. James found himself smiling as he watched her.

"Objection!"

"Mrs. Ashwood, watch yourself," the judge said, and then advised Mr. Bassetti not to answer.

Mak walked toward Mr. Bassetti—slow, stalking steps. She stood right in front of him, and James witnessed the change in his body language—a subtle leaning back, a tight drawing of his shoulders. She was intimidating him, and it was clear he didn't like it.

"Mr. Bassetti, you're a proud man, aren't you? A man who has become very successful, and very powerful. And the more powerful you became, the more careless you became. You thought you were invincible, so imagine your surprise when you discovered Ms. Nelson had been quietly taping you, quietly documenting your every move." Mak leaned in. "Imagine, your favorite girl, the one you had given so much to, turned on you and you had no idea. She betrayed you, gave your secrets to others. She knew you would kill her if you found out, so she made sure she wasn't the only one who knew."

"She was a whore, not a mastermind," Mr. Bassetti said.

"A whore? That's a very degrading term, Mr. Bassetti," Mak said.

"She degraded herself!"

"Did she? Is that how you justified beating the last breath out of her? Did she deserve to die?" Mak said, raising her voice.

"Yes, she's a whore that deserved to die!" Mr. Bassetti spat out in a heated exchange. "But I didn't kill her, Mrs. Ashwood."

"I don't believe you. I think she was a threat to your ego, to your empire built on crime and violence. She made a fool of you, and you punished her for it."

"Objection!"

"Withdrawn. No further questions, Your Honor," Mak said, staring at Mr. Bassetti.

She was brilliant. A perfect blend of sweet and evil that had captured the entire courtroom. Even James found himself leaning toward the computer, drawn to the screen. There was one major problem, though: Mak was humiliating this man, and like Ms. Nelson and her friends, it would be a miracle if they didn't punish her too.

James watched as Mak went back to her seat. He wanted to tell her he was proud of her, but he'd promised himself from now on he'd treat her just like any other client—he'd engage with her as little as possible.

He packed up the laptop and listened for Deacon's cue to come through his earpiece. He was in an office they had secured within the courthouse, close enough to get to her if needed. Samuel had already advised there was a media storm outside, which concerned James.

"Moving," Deacon said.

James counted to ten and then stepped into the hallway. His coordination with Deacon was seamless, and he walked directly behind them, hidden by the cluster of people between them. James had instructed Cami to keep Mak moving and to get her straight into the car. It sounded logical and easy, but in reality, when there were that many people waiting to get a comment or photograph of her, it was far from either. Deacon lagged behind and fell into pace beside James, and they exited the building, waiting behind the columns for Mak's car to leave. Their car then pulled up, and they followed the first car back to Mak's office. Timing was everything, and so far they hadn't made a mistake.

The rest of the evening was uneventful and when Mak was back in her apartment at Thomas Security, James went to see Samuel for his daily update.

"I found something today, something you're not going to like,"

Samuel said as James sat down, eyeing the late-night dinner spread on the table. He took a box of noodles.

"Keep talking," James said.

"I've been working on who might've slipped Mak that note. You have to book online for those classes, and one of the women didn't check out. The studio has a security system, but it only monitors the door and stairwell. I was able to get a picture of each person entering, though, and check the identification against the list of names. This is her," Samuel said, loading a woman's photograph on the screen. "I was then able to track her on some CCTV footage leaving the studio. She was walking, probably home, when she got into a white car six blocks from the studio. Unfortunately I can't get a clear read on the plate. Since she got into that car, I haven't been able to find any further movement of her—no credit card transactions, no mobile calls, nothing. And then this evening, I got a database hit—her roommate reported her missing about an hour ago."

James groaned. "Do you think they paid her to give Mak the note, and then took her to prevent her from talking?"

"That's exactly what I think happened," Samuel said. "I can't find anything else at this stage, but I believe we can be absolutely certain that these guys aren't going to play nice. I would be surprised if that young lady isn't already dead.

"I have some other news, too. Shall I continue?" Samuel asked.

James raised his eyebrows—Samuel had certainly had a productive day. "Please do."

"This is about you. The four Escanta guys you killed in Hungary. Well, you only killed three, but the fourth is dead because of you, so we'll just include him in this," Samuel said, getting to the point at a pace that was annoying James, but he said nothing. "I set up a code to track any correlating data from their cell phones, credit card transactions, airplane tickets, et cetera. I got a hit this morning. In the past three years, all of them have stayed at the Docoss Hotel in London. It's a legit, swanky hotel, but I'm wondering if it's a favorite of the Escanta boys for a reason. Perhaps they have an arrangement with management? I'm sorting through financial records, but you know how these things go . . . groups like Escanta don't usually pay via traceable means, so I doubt I'm going to find anything. I think you might need to make a reservation and have a friendly chat with the manager." Samuel sat down, apparently done with his revelations.

James knew that Samuel was right, and he should go, but he didn't want to leave Mak right now. "It's going to have to wait," he said.

Samuel tapped his hands on the table. "I thought you might say that. I don't have any other leads, James. These guys are careful, so damn careful. We're not going to get many chances like this."

James had never hesitated to follow a lead, but her case was heating up and it could erupt at any time. "The hotel isn't going anywhere."

"Perhaps not, but management could. The one person who knows something could disappear if we leave it too long. There is also a chance it's already too late." Samuel shrugged his shoulders.

"Her trial will finish soon. These guys are kidnapping and likely murdering anyone who might incriminate them, so I can't leave right now. We'll wait it out a few weeks. Get a list of all of the staff and known associates and run reports on them. At least if they disappear I'll have something to work from," James said and then added, "if they're not dead by the time I get to them."

"All right, I'll work on it," Samuel said, looking over the remaining dinner options.

"Anything else?" James asked.

Samuel looked both amused and offended. "What? That wasn't good enough for you? Do you think I'm special and get thirty hours in a day or something?"

James cracked a smile. "Hey, I'm just checking—no need to be so touchy."

"Sometimes you boys think I can work miracles. You drive like *maniacs*, which takes me hours of video editing to cover up, and then you expect me to have answers for all your questions a few days later . . . geez, I don't know," Samuel said with a glint of humor in his eyes.

"*Maniacs,*" James repeated, chuckling to himself. Mak had yet to see the definition of a maniac. "At least that's better than being told you're irritating," James said, just to get a laugh out of Samuel—and it worked.

"Did you look through the list of apartments I sent you?" Samuel asked.

James shook his head. "I'll do it tonight."

"You're going to have to think about an explanation for the rent—she's going to know she can't afford such an apartment. I've been watching our footage of her in the courtroom. She's very good. She should be working in the private sector—she'd be earning at least five times what she is now. But I understand why she chose the path she did."

Mak's morals and beliefs came before income, and James admired that. A lot of people will do just about anything for money. Some might assume he'd made that choice, but oddly enough he'd done some terrible things for very little money. Military and agency wages weren't high, and he'd made all of his money since starting Thomas Security—it was an unbelievably lucrative business model.

"I was thinking of telling her that, due to the number of clients we've rented apartments for, we get a subsidized rate. Do you think that'll fly?" James asked, smirking.

Samuel's lips wiggled from side to side as he thought it through. "Questionable. But I don't know what else you can tell her. Just prepare yourself for a barrage of questions. Do you think she was like that as a child? She must have driven her parents mad."

"Do you know what surprises me? Her husband managed to live a lie, right under her nose. Was she either not paying any attention to him, or was he just a brilliant liar?" James questioned, thinking aloud.

"That is interesting. Both, maybe?"

"Any follow-up on his actions abroad?" James asked.

"No, but I haven't had time to look into it much further. I didn't think it was a priority," Samuel said.

"It's not, I'm just interested to see what that guy was up to." Part of him wanted to see what her husband had been up to, and the other didn't—sometimes you were better off not knowing. "I'm worried about that money, though."

"Why? It's been sitting there for years," Samuel said casually.

"Exactly. Someone with dirty hands paid that money to him, and people with dirty hands know how to find money. It's sitting in bank accounts in his name. How come it hasn't been moved? It would be easy to do, right?" James finished the last of his noodles and tucked the flaps of the box back in before he threw it into the trash.

"It would be easy for me to do," Samuel said pointedly. "But not necessarily easy for someone else."

"I still think it's odd that it hasn't been touched. Criminals like their money, they love it, and they'll take any chance possible to get back a bad debt."

Samuel sat quietly for a moment. "They surely can't be waiting for her to claim it. It's been years, and we know how impatient criminals are."

"Mmm, I don't know what to make of it other than it doesn't make sense." Nothing was making sense to James today, and that worried him. He wasn't a worrier—thoughtful, yes, but not a worrier. He dealt with problems as they arose, piece by piece. But he found himself worried about Mak. Initially he'd thought it was because she was so unable to protect herself, unlike Deacon and Cami. But Samuel was probably the most vulnerable of all due to his skillset and James didn't worry about him—although his unusual lifestyle made that all the more possible.

Samuel never left Thomas Security. Never. He had everything delivered and for fresh air and his daily dose of vitamin D he went into one of the courtyards for a period of time each day. James had once gently reminded him that the building wasn't a prison and he was free to come and go but, for whatever reason, he liked to stay inside. And that solved James's problem of protecting him, so he didn't argue about it. Samuel was a truly weird genius.

"On another note completely," Samuel said, "I bought you some more shares this morning. Well, I bought Patrick some shares."

James laughed. In the financial world, James Thomas was Patrick McCormack. Patrick owned the majority of his cash and assets.

"I think it will turn out to be a very profitable buy," Samuel said with a wink.

Samuel also doubled as his investment banker. James didn't ask questions on Samuel's methods for selecting and purchasing stocks, but he had yet to pick a loser—at least of the purchases he intended to make money on. Some shares he bought intending to lose money so that his trading activities wouldn't draw any unwanted attention— Samuel took insider trading to a whole new level.

"Thank you, Samuel," James said, chuckling. "I can go shopping now."

Samuel laughed as he stood and tidied up the remnants of dinner. James helped him and when the desk was clear and the table wiped down, they closed up Samuel's office.

Samuel lived in the apartment next to the one Mak was staying in. James said goodbye from the elevator and then continued up one floor.

He took a long, hot shower, and turned in for the night. He would need his sleep, because tomorrow had a different plan for him.

16

MAK ASHWOOD

Twenty-four hours. It was the time Mak estimated was left in the trial. And then any period of time it might take the jury to reach a verdict. Had she done enough? Had she pressed the witnesses hard enough? Had she missed a fact or a piece of evidence? Her mind spun like an amusement park ride, and she couldn't get it to stop. This was it—the chance for the victims and their families to get justice—and the responsibility sat heavily on her shoulders.

But even with all the angst in her mind, there was hope, and pride, too. She could possibly pull this off. She could win, and she could give justice to those who had paid the ultimate price, and for their families whose hearts were still bleeding. And she could say "fuck you" to all the doubters.

Mak had just finished a late meeting with her assistant prosecutor and her personal assistant. They were ready for tomorrow, and she was going to fight until the very last word of the rebuttal. *You can do this*. Mak gave herself a little pep talk as she looked out of the car window. Cami sat beside her in the back seat, and another bodyguard and driver were in the front.

The car was silent, until it wasn't anymore. A flapping noise increased in intensity as the car continued to speed along.

"Go through the next intersection," Cami said. Her voice, and even her words, were mundane but she drew her weapon, which was something Mak had never seen her do.

"Code Six," Cami said, and the two men in the front, in unison, said, "Copy."

"Mak," Cami said, "we've got a flat tire, and we need to change cars. Deacon is behind us, and in a few seconds they're going to—"

Cami went mute, and her head snapped up, looking to Mak's right.

Mak yelped as Cami grabbed her arms, steadying her as a clapping bang echoed in Mak's ears. Their car jolted to the left, threatening to flip over on its side as they were rammed by another car.

"Code Blue!" Cami yelled.

What is code blue? Mak opened her mouth to speak, but an explosion stilled the words in her throat and panic took on a whole new meaning.

The car door opened and Mak was pulled from the car. It happened so fast, and her mind couldn't keep up with what was happening. Either the shock, or the panic, or both, had left her startled and dumbfounded.

Mak's adrenaline came to the party late, but when it did she found strength she didn't know existed. She fought back the arms that were holding her as he carried her into the construction site of a new building.

"Stop it!" James said, pushing her up against a dusty wall and covering her mouth with his hand. "Shh." His eyes were serious and threatening and she struggled to breathe through her nose. There was too much adrenaline rocketing through her body and not enough air to calm her mind. "I need to listen, so be quiet," he said.

Mak nodded her head, and he took his hand away from her mouth. She drew in deep breaths while trying to work out what was happening. She followed his eyes as they darted from point to point, but he gave away nothing.

"Let's go," he said, pulling her hand as they ran through the building. The moonlight diminished the farther into the building they went, and Mak stumbled a few times—her heels were not made for running through construction sites—but James kept her upright and moving forward. She squinted, trying to see where they were going, but they were moving too fast with not enough light. And in the dark, everything seemed heightened. Her panting breath seemed louder, the touch of his hand felt electric, the scent of his cologne floating behind him like an invisible trail was intoxicating. The darkness over-whelmed her senses.

"Second point," James said as they ran, and Mak wondered who the hell he was talking to. He came to a halt, tucked her body behind him with one arm, and then fired a bullet. Mak screamed, crouching behind his body.

He pulled her in front of him now, grabbing both of her upper arms like he was going to shake her. The calmness of his voice was in juxtaposition to the situation. "I'm going to get you out of this, and we're going to be fine. But don't scream, don't say a word, and do everything I say. Okay?"

Mak wished she could see his face but his voice alone was surpris-ingly comforting. "Yes," she said.

And then he swung a door—one that Mak hadn't even been able to see—open, took her hand and they ran out into a passageway so narrow that Mak's flailing arm grazed on the rough brick of the wall. She knew she'd taken a layer of skin off but in that moment she felt no pain. She could, however, hear her heart drumming in her ears and her legs felt that strange, tingly combination of light and heavy.

James slowed them down as they neared the street, but he kept hold of her hand. "Copy," he said, talking to his imaginary friend again.

It was slightly lighter in the passageway, and she could make out the features of his face. He looked just like he did every day—calm and in control. "Walk beside me now, don't run, and keep your back against the wall, okay?"

"Yes," Mak said.

He squeezed her hand, nodded his head and then pulled her out onto the street. They walked for three blocks, their shoulders scraping against the walls. Mak had so many questions burning in her mind, begging to be spoken, but she kept her lips shut tight —for now.

As they neared the corner of the block, he stopped again. "We're going into that hotel." He tilted his head toward the building diagonally across the street. "There's no cover, so we need to run. Or rather, I need to run and shield you. I'm going to hold you to my front and make a dash for it. We'll be safe inside there, I promise. Ready?"

"What do you mean, hold me?"

"Don't scream," James said as he lifted her into one arm and started sprinting diagonally across the intersection. He pushed the entrance door and they were suddenly standing on a black-and-white tiled floor, in a lobby drowning in flowers. Mak felt like she'd fallen down a rabbit hole and into a magical garden.

James put her down, looked her over, and then took her hand. He led her up to the check-in desk. "One room for Jones, please," he said.

The man behind the desk gave a smile that hid a thousand secrets. "It's a pleasure to have you stay again, Mr. Jones," he said warmly. "Floor fifteen, room seventeen. Is there anything you'll require for your stay?" He placed two black cards on the counter and slid them toward James.

"No, thank you, not now." James tucked the cards into his back pocket and then leisurely led Mak to the elevator.

"Mr. Jones?" Mak whispered as they stood side by side, waiting for the elevator to arrive.

"Shh," James said, with no further explanation.

The elevator was empty when it arrived, but James still didn't offer an explanation. When he closed the room door, he bolted it and then turned to Mak, looking her over properly now. He turned her around like a puppet, 180 degrees, and then in a full 360 to face him. He looked at her bleeding arm, the result of the wall graze in the passageway.

"Let's clean that," he said, taking her hand again.

He led her into the bathroom and when he opened the vanity

cabinet, Mak was surprised to see it was stocked with medical supplies.

"What is this place?" Mak said with wide eyes.

"A hotel—a special hotel," James said without looking at her. He was searching through the medical supplies and pulled out several white packages. He then washed his hands and opened the first package containing a white cloth.

He wrapped his hand underneath her upper arm and gently washed the graze with warm water and a liquid solution from a bottle that had also come from the cabinet.

"What is going on? What happened tonight?" Mak asked, growing impatient with the lack of communication. He was giving her a trickle of information, and she wanted a stream of flowing words from his mouth.

"I don't exactly know. That car collision wasn't an accident—that much I'm sure of. I think it's safe to assume it's the same people that have been sending you notes. I'll know more once we get back to Thomas Security."

He patted her graze dry with the cotton cloth, but she noted he still hadn't looked into her eyes. Not once.

He squeezed a small amount of white cream from a tube and carefully, expertly, spread it over the scrape. It still didn't hurt, and Mak wasn't sure if that was due to the shock or the fact that his touch was distracting from the pain.

James tore open another package to reveal a bandage.

"Most hotels don't come stocked with medical supplies," Mak said with a pointed look that his downcast eyes didn't see.

"I've told you already, this is a special hotel. That's all you need to know," he said, wrapping up her arm. He secured the bandage, washed his hands again and then dried them with the hand towel.

He was avoiding making eye contact, and Mak had grown tired of it.

"James," she said, waiting until he looked at her.

When his eyes met hers, the barrier was down, and for the first time she could truly see the want in his eyes. She hadn't imagined it

—he was affected by her. His chest heaved, and she felt her body mirror his. He looked away quickly.

"James," Mak repeated.

"Mak, don't."

Mak ignored him, taking a step forward, closing the space between them. He seemed to sigh in resignation. He pressed his hand to his ear, and then closed his eyes.

"I can't do this, Mak—I can't get involved with you. I can't get involved with anyone." He pressed his lips together and shook his head. "It's not safe . . . This, us, is a very bad idea. And I'm not the man you think I am, Mak. You only know one side of me and the other side, well, believe me you would not like it."

"I'm not sure I agree with that," Mak said. "I'm usually a very good judge of character. Granted, we've barely had the chance to get to know each other, but I would like to know more."

"That's the problem, you can only ever know one part of me—one side of who I am, the side that's safe for you to see, and the side I want you to see. The other side—that person you can never know. You don't have all of the information about me that you should, and I can't tell you because it'll put you in danger."

"Which part of that are you more worried about? Me not knowing you, or your past putting me in danger?" Mak asked.

"Both."

"Why can't you protect me from your past? That is what Thomas Security does, right? And you got us here safely tonight."

He exhaled a long breath. "There are no guarantees in this game, and things happen that are beyond our control. And just because I got you out tonight doesn't mean that I'll always be able to protect you. I could create the most detailed, resource-intensive security plan for you and still it might not be good enough. If you understood the gravity of my past, you would understand." He looked straight into her eyes. "I've thought about it every day since I met you, wondering if it was possible to make this work, but it's not. I want what's best for you, and that's just not me."

"Don't make a decision yet," Mak said, trying to buy some more time to persuade him.

Mak was a gambler. She took on high-risk cases because she liked the challenge, as much as they troubled her. And obviously her choice in men was no different. He was a risk, one she knew little about, but whatever his past, she wanted the chance to get to know him.

"I've already made the decision," he said.

"So un-make it. The issue about me not knowing who you truly are, that's a risk I'm willing to take. And I think you can protect me . . . but I think you're scared," Mak said.

"With good reason," he muttered under his breath. He rested both hands on the vanity, leaning forward on his straight arms. He looked deep into her eyes, seeming to search for something. Fear? Hesitation? Calling her bluff?

Eventually he spoke again. "A relationship with me would be very different. I couldn't take the risk of getting to know you, even going out on a few casual dates without putting into place stringent security measures. And you would *hate* the security measures I would want to employ."

Mak cleared her throat. "Well, that's something we would have to discuss."

"There would be no discussion about it. There would be a set of rules, and measures put in place, and the only say you would have in it would be to agree to follow them. How appealing does that sound?"

Mak swallowed. It didn't sound appealing, but she still wanted to have the conversation. "I'm prepared to hear them."

James groaned, looking away again, and Mak took the opportunity to close the remaining space between them. She took another step forward and held his long fingers in her small hand. He didn't tell her to stop, and he didn't push her away, but he did curse under his breath.

"Don't make this decision yet. Let's get to know each other while I'm under your security anyway, and that way we can at least talk about the security issue," Mak said.

He looked down at their hands and the energy shifted between them.

"How did you become so good at breaking people down?" he asked.

She smiled. "It's a natural talent honed with experience."

Mak knew she'd played the right cards, and her heart drummed wildly as she waited for him to make the next move.

He threaded his fingers through hers and wrapped them around her waist, drawing her in. He paused, and Mak thought he might change his mind, but he didn't pull away. She tilted her chin up, and he brought his lips to hers, kissing her for the first time.

Mak's chest fluttered, and she opened her mouth wider, letting his tongue dip in, brushing over hers. She wrapped her arms around him, squeezing him to her.

She heard him groan, a guttural noise solicited from deep in his chest.

His back tensed as her fingers trailed over his thin sweater. She could feel his muscles move, her fingers creating a ripple as they traced his spine. He lifted her up, sitting her on the vanity as he continued to kiss her.

When he finally pulled back, their breathing was labored, heavier than it had ever been while they were running to the hotel.

"I can't believe I'm doing this," he mumbled, and Mak thought he really did look astonished. It was rare to see him portray such raw emotions.

His eyes flickered, his face resumed its composed look, and he pressed his ear and said, "Copy."

"*Who* are you talking to?"

He pressed his ear again. "Samuel, Deacon, Cami . . . everyone. I have an earpiece in, and when I squeeze it I can turn mute on and off. Look, we don't have much time. Deacon's on his way over to pick us up."

"No—tell him to wait," Mak said.

"I can't. The team created a diversion so I could get you out of the car without being seen. I need to check that everyone's okay and then debrief." He sighed. "We need to talk about this, and you really need time to think it all over. You have adrenaline in your body, and you're in the middle of a huge trial, and right now is not the time to be a making a decision like this. And I need to know I gave you time to really consider what 'we' would mean.

"You might think you know who I am, Mak, but you don't. I used to justify my career, my actions, because I was given orders for them. But then I saw too much. And I decided to punish those men that used me to do their dirty work. I became the kind of man you despise, and I made a lot of enemies in the process," he said, visibly swallowing.

"You need to understand that that is all I will ever be able to tell you, and that your life would be at risk by being my girlfriend. You really need to think about that when you have a clear head and aren't reacting to the moment. When your trial is over we'll talk, and if you change your mind there will be no hard feelings. In fact I pray to God you change your mind," James said, shaking his head.

"Until then," he continued, "this stays between us. Deacon and I have a few rules, one of them is no girlfriends, for several reasons—one of which being it complicates things greatly. I will talk to him and deal with this, but I'm not going to do that until you're sure this is what you want."

"Okay," Mak said. *Baby steps.*

"We need to go downstairs," he said, but instead of moving away he drew her in closer. He gazed down at her, brushing a strand of hair from her eyes. He leaned in and kissed her, letting his lips brush over hers. He closed his eyes, and Mak did the same, letting her soul fall into the kiss.

"Now we really need to go downstairs," he said with a sexy smirk. He took her hand, picking up the room keys as he led her out of the room and toward the elevator.

The elevator doors opened and he shuffled her in. There were two other guests in the elevator, so they didn't speak, but he kept her close to his side.

When they reached the lobby floor he waited for the guests to exit and then they walked up to the same desk they had just checked in at.

"Checking out. Thank you for your hospitality," James said.

The man nodded once. "It is always our pleasure to have you, Mr. Jones."

No money was exchanged, nor were any personal details, but from the interaction between the two men it was clear this was not James Thomas's first stay.

They walked toward the lobby and Mak whispered the same question he'd refused to answer before. "Mr. Jones?"

"I have many names, Mak, but James Thomas is my favorite," he said under his breath.

Mak was greeted by a group of ten men and ushered into a waiting car before she had a chance to ask the question in her mind: *Why was James Thomas his favorite?*

He slid in next to her and the car pulled away before he barely had the door closed.

"How are you doing, Mak?"

Mak craned her head to see the driver—the same man who addressed her. It was Deacon.

"I'm fine. How is everyone? Is Cami okay?"

"She's perfectly fine. Everyone got out unscathed," he said, his eyes meeting hers in the rearview mirror.

"Good," she said, relieved.

Neither James nor Deacon spoke again. And James didn't touch her; if anything, he sat as far away from her as possible.

When they arrived at Thomas Security, the tension seemed to drop as they pulled up. And in the safety of their parking lot, there was less of a flurry getting Mak out of the car.

"I'll take Mak to her apartment and then meet you in Samuel's office," James said once they were in the elevator. He pressed two buttons on the elevator panel. Deacon got out at the first stop and Mak noted the floor level—ten. They continued up to Mak's apartment.

James unlocked the apartment for her and closed the door

behind them. "I'm going to be in Samuel's office for the next few hours, debriefing and working out what happened tonight. Do you need anything before I leave?"

"No, I'm fine," Mak said.

"Are you sure you're okay? A lot happened tonight, and you haven't had a chance to decompress from any of it."

Mak nodded her head. "Yeah, I'm fine," she said honestly. Maybe she was in shock, or maybe it was the truth, because she felt safe with him, and she felt safe in this building.

"I have to get downstairs," he said, drawing her in once more. "Try and get some sleep, but call me if you need anything at all."

"Sure," she said, nodding her head.

He seemed hesitant to leave, and she didn't want him to either. He brought his lips to hers, and she opened her mouth for him, melting into his arms as he kissed her. But it was a short-lived kiss. "I need to go before they turn on the cameras in here and see this," he said.

"When are we going to talk?" Mak asked as he began to walk away.

"Soon."

17

JAMES THOMAS

His dream team was settled in Samuel's office for what was going to be a long night.

"Who is hurt?" James asked immediately. It was impossible, with a situation like they'd experienced tonight, for someone not to be hurt. Hopefully no one was dead. But he was glad Deacon had had the sense to lie to Mak about it.

"Tommy's got a flesh wound—medics are treating it—and there are a few other glass and shrapnel wounds but everyone's looking good," Deacon said, pulling out a chair for him.

"What the fuck happened to that tire?" James asked.

"A nail took it out," Cami said. "A nail conveniently placed. We went back and had a look, they were scattered over all of our possible exit routes."

Mak's driver changed routes nearly every night, in order not to be predictable, so the assholes had to litter all of the streets. There were going to be a lot of flat tires in Manhattan over the next twenty-four hours.

As soon as the tire had blown, James had called the first code. He'd been in the car behind, and his instincts told him something was very wrong. The initial code plan had been to change her into his car. Until her car was rammed from the side. Samuel had given them warning, enough to stop Mak from being crushed, but they didn't get any luckier than that.

James then called a diversion code. His team played out a scene they'd rehearsed hundreds of times, and used a couple of times. His men fell into grids, blocking off and zoning the site. And then they ushered Cami into Deacon's car, making it look like it was Mak, while James snatched her from the other side of the car. None of it would've been possible without the flashbangs they'd set off. They'd effectively dazzled their enemies and bought a few precious seconds. Taking Mak on his own was a risk, but he'd used this strategy several times before, and it had never failed him. And he knew he was just blocks from Hotel Tivoli—a safe house for men like him. There was one strict rule in that hotel, and that was that no one was to be harmed. Ever. If you did, the punishment was the death penalty, and they didn't give you a quick injection to end your life.

James looked at Samuel, who in return eyed him suspiciously. Samuel knew that something had happened between James and Mak. Samuel wouldn't have accessed Hotel Tivoli's cameras—that was one of the few systems he would never hack—but he would've known James was turning his earpiece on and off mute. And that spoke volumes—particularly given he never did that.

"What do we know about the men in the car?"

"Three men were in the car, and another firing from a motorbike behind them," Samuel said, clarifying. "Americans. But all have visited Italy in the last eighteen months. This one, though," Samuel said, loading a photograph onto one of the screens, "is Special Forces. Or was Special Forces but is apparently running in a different group now. The other three are dead, but he escaped."

James chewed on his cheek—that was news he didn't want to hear.

"He made a sudden departure, and we lost him," Samuel said, pushing his glasses up the ridge of his nose.

"When did the mob start inducting Special Forces guys?" James asked. The Camarro mob was traditionalist, especially the old boys.

They were renowned for recruiting through extended family and close associates. And the more Italian blood you had, the better. James could see just by looking at this guy's photograph that very little, if any, Italian blood flowed through his veins.

"I was thinking the same thing," Deacon said. "Something's not right about this."

"Maybe they've had to adapt," Cami suggested. "Times have changed and to be competitive they need guys like him."

"Maybe," James said, unconvinced. "Keep working on this, Samuel. I want to know what other ties they have to the Italian mob other than making a trip or two to Italy.

"By the way, what's the damage estimate?" James asked, screwing up his nose. He didn't even want to know the answer. Last year their insurance premiums had become so expensive it had essentially deemed them uninsurable. It was cheaper now just to pay for the damage outright.

"Several hundred thousand at least. You have two damaged cars, one of which is going to be a write-off," Samuel said, shifting in his chair. "The car chase and now this . . . You're attracting way too much attention." He looked at James when he said this—too much attention, and therefore too much cover-up, created too many questions by the wrong men. And gossip traveled faster in a criminal circle than it did in a women's knitting club.

"She's becoming very expensive," Deacon said pointedly.

James shrugged his shoulders. "Well, we charge our other clients ludicrous prices so think of her as our good deed for the year."

They spent the next two hours going over further details and designing a new security plan for tomorrow. When James was finally confident in their strategy, he suggested everyone get some sleep. They all piled into the elevator and said their goodnights as Samuel and Cami exited on their floor. James and Deacon rode up one more level, and Deacon seemed relieved that James didn't get out on the floor below.

"Night," James said, unlocking his apartment.

Instead of going to bed, though, he made a cup of tea and sat at his kitchen island, staring at the speckled granite bench top. They were missing something, and he knew it.

Death is but an illusion, as you will soon see.

Keep your eyes open, Makaela.

Contact. Wait out.

Only the third note made sense to him, and they hadn't had to wait long for the enemy to attack. James wasn't sure that was their big move, though—he had a feeling it was only the prelude.

Either the mob had indeed starting recruiting Special Forces guys, or someone else was targeting her. But why? James couldn't find one viable motive. If she had touched the money, it would make sense, but the money sat dormant in the bank accounts. James didn't believe that whoever was the payee of those deposits didn't know where it was, even if it had been shuffled from other bank accounts. Creative accounting wouldn't hide six million dollars from a criminal in an account in Eric's name. He'd never intended to hide it, James was sure of that, and that fact alone didn't make sense.

James himself never had money, or even bank accounts, in the alias he used in his everyday life—James Thomas didn't exist on paper. And never, ever, would he put money into an account in his birth name.

But if it wasn't about the money, the only other reasonable explanation was her trial—the mob. It was unlikely, but it was possible they were recruiting Special Forces guys. Or maybe they contract them—that would be a more feasible explanation given the Camarro boys' heritage.

Contracting in the underworld was a good way of making money, and it was what James and Deacon had done before Samuel found them. They had initially fled to Asia, where no one knew them, and job by job they built up a considerable cash reserve. It was there he'd first met Kyoji Tohmatsu. He had been one of the most well-connected criminals James had ever met. And one of the most dangerous.

Their lives changed in Tokyo. It had been their fresh start, but after Nicole's death, Tokyo was a city of loss for Deacon. And they couldn't go back to Europe, so they headed for the land of opportunity—America.

James traced the swirling cluster of speckles on the bench top with his index finger as he thought.

So many different, seemingly unconnected, events had shaped their lives in ways he could never have imagined. And his gut feeling told him Mak's entrance into their lives was going to do the same. He had that sense of impending change, that something life-altering was waiting in his destiny. And it wasn't a good feeling. He liked boredom. He liked mundane. He liked calm days and nights.

He didn't fear the unknown, but he feared losing the life he'd come to love.

18

MAK ASHWOOD

Mak's eyes passed over the jury. An odd sense of completion, yet the need to do more, overcame her. She'd delivered her closing argument and rebuttal, and now the fate of Mr. Bassetti was out of her hands. It was in the hands of the men and women in front of her, and she could only pray they reached the right decision.

Mak sat down in her seat, catching the eye of the defense lawyer. She liked him as little as she liked the defendant, of whom she considered the scum of this earth and the downfall of humankind.

She'd listened to his predictable arguments, and kept her poker face on even when she really wanted to reveal what she was thinking. She'd wondered again what Mr. Bassetti was paying this man. It was likely in the millions, but that money came with a cost—defending men like him. They say everyone has a price but Mak disagreed—you could never pay her enough to defend such a man.

The judge began his charge—the reading of the instructions to the jury—and then the jury retired for deliberation.

That's it, I can't do anything else. She noticed a slight trembling of her hands, an anxious reaction as she watched the jury exit from the courtroom. She packed up her notes and stole a look at her assistant prosecutor—he looked calm and collected, but he, too, had a good poker face: it was a requirement of the profession.

"Let's go," Mak said, immediately noticing she'd used the same words James Thomas loved to use. She hadn't seen him since he'd walked her up to her apartment and kissed her goodbye. If not for the weight of her trial, she doubted she'd have been able to get him out of her mind today, but her focus had been on other things—it had to be.

Cami flanked her side as they exited the courtroom. Mak made eye-contact with the each of the victims' parents who were present and sitting together, and had been for the entire trial. She gave them a confident smile and a nod of her head, but otherwise she didn't stop to talk to them. They all knew nothing more could be said today, and Mak wasn't going to offer any false reassurances—that wouldn't help anyone if the verdicts came back not guilty.

"We'll go back to the office. There's no telling how long the jury might take to reach the verdicts," Mak said to Cami as they walked side-by-side.

"Sure," Cami said.

As they reached the front entrance to the courthouse, Mak was joined by five other bodyguards. Mak looked to Cami for an explanation.

"The result of last night," she said, shrugging her shoulders. Cami spoke little when they were in public.

In a perfectly-timed coordination, Mak's car arrived as her heel lifted off the last step and onto the pavement. She was ushered inside, where she finally closed her eyes and dropped the act.

She kept them closed all the way to her office. She was not in the mood to make small talk—she wasn't in the mood to talk at all. The trip passed quickly, and she went straight to her office and closed the door. She sat at her desk and hung her head in her hands, exhaling the tension that had taken hostage of her body over the past few months. *You did everything you could,* Mak told herself, but the words weren't as comforting as she would've liked.

Mak sat there, still and quiet, but her mind was busy reflecting. It didn't help to look back on the trial now, but she couldn't help herself.

She jumped, startled, when her office phone rang.

"Mak Ashwood," she answered.

"How are you doing?"

James's voice was deep but comforting.

"The suspense is killing me," Mak admitted. "I'm questioning everything, I . . ." Her voice trailed off.

"I've been told you were brilliant," James said.

Mak scoffed. "Who told you that?"

"Cami. And Deacon."

"They're biased," Mak said.

"No, they're not at all. If any two people love to speak the truth, believe me it's them," James said with a light chuckle.

Mak smiled. Thomas Security must be a very interesting place to be a fly on the wall. "Well, I'll take the compliment, but it doesn't matter what we think, does it? It only matters what that jury thinks."

"Mmm. Regardless of what the jury thinks, I think you should be proud. I'm proud of you, Mak. Few lawyers would've taken that case, particularly at this stage of your career, and you know it. And you've had to deal with this security mess on top everything else."

"Thank you," she said quietly—she'd never been good at taking compliments. "Where are you?"

"Not very far from you," James said and Mak could almost hear his smile in his words.

"Are you always so close?" Mak bit her lip—this call had become a good distraction for her mind.

"Almost always. And if you were to become my girlfriend, I'll become a shadow you might wish would disappear every now and then."

"You would follow me everywhere, even when this case is over?" Mak rocked back in her chair, wrapping the telephone cord around her fingers.

"Yes, I, or someone, would follow you everywhere. You would never be completely alone again," James said, completely serious.

That thought was very unappealing to Mak—she was used to being alone. "I have to be alone sometimes, otherwise I might end up in the defendant's seat."

"You can't be. I told you, Mak, you will need to think about this very carefully."

"You left me alone last night," Mak pointed out.

"Well, Thomas Security is a different scenario. And, anyway, every room in that building has surveillance, so you're not completely alone."

"I see," Mak said. It was weird to know her every move could be watched on camera, but at the same time she rarely thought about the cameras. Her mind had been consumed with the trial, though, and so maybe that would change now.

"So, I've been giving this, us, some thought today. And while you are staying at Thomas Security, it does present an opportunity for us to get to know each other. I still don't think it's a good idea for us to talk about things until your trial is over, but I was thinking, if you're up for it, that you should come to my apartment when you're done at the office."

"I want to, but . . . my mind is distracted, James. I probably won't be very good company."

"I don't care, and you don't have to pretend with me. If talking about the trial will help, we can do that. Or we can watch a movie or something to help you relax. Whatever you want. But what are you going to do otherwise? Sit in the apartment and drive yourself crazy?"

It was exactly what she had planned to do. "Okay."

"Good. I'll come and get you from your apartment. I'll see you later."

"Bye, James," Mak said, placing the phone back down on the receiver.

Mak's assistant, Amanda, walked in. *Surely not already.* Mak panicked.

"I'm going to order us some dinner," Amanda said, and Mak breathed a sigh of relief. A verdict that quick meant either an epic win or an epic fail.

"What would you like?" Amanda asked, tapping her pen on her yellow notepad.

"I don't think I can stomach anything," Mak said, shaking her head.

"I'll get you a smoothie or something."

"Thanks," Mak said, but she doubted she'd even drink it.

Mak was nervously picking at the cuticles of her nails when James walked in. It was a bad habit, and one she had to stop, otherwise they might end up bleeding.

"Relax," he said as he walked toward her. He tilted her chin up, and she placed her hands on his chest. Her stomach fluttered, and she was glad he was here with her. Sometimes being alone was very hard.

She leaned in to kiss him and saw a smile on his lips before they met hers. His mouth tasted like sweet spearmint, and his lips were soft as they pressed against hers.

"Let's go," he said, uttering his two favorite words.

Mak smiled. "Do you realize how often you say that?"

James cracked a smile too. "I'm always moving. Come on."

They took the stairs up one level to his apartment. James went through a rigorous system to unlock his door, which seemed insanely ridiculous given the building they were in.

"Why so many tests?" Mak asked, eyeing the retina scanner.

"Just because." He winked at her. He shuffled her inside and turned on the lights. His apartment looked similar to the one she was staying in, just a little larger. And it looked as empty. Emptier, even.

"Where are all your belongings?" Mak said, looking at the sparse surroundings. No books, no photos, no collectibles of any kind.

"I don't have a lot of stuff," James said.

"You don't have anything," Mak corrected.

"I have clothes in my closet, amenities in my bathroom, and food in my kitchen—that's all I need. Now, what would you like to do tonight?"

Mak craned her head around the pillar to look at what she thought should be the entertainment unit in the living room. It, too, was empty.

James smiled. "I have a television in my bedroom. But if you want to watch a movie I think we should go to the movie theatre downstairs," he said. "It even comes with a popcorn machine."

"You have a movie theatre?" *What else does Thomas Security have hidden in this building?*

"Well, it's a home cinema—not a full theatre—but, yes. We like to leave this building as little as possible."

"Perhaps you should give me a tour of the entire building."

James gave her a mischievous grin. "I'll save that for another day."

Mak laughed, thinking she would never get the full tour of his building.

"Do you want to watch a movie?" James asked.

Mak nodded. "Sure."

"Let's go," he said, taking her hand. They took the elevator express to B1, and when they stepped out he led her down a wide corridor, stopping at a set of double doors. He entered another code, unlocking the room. It seemed every room in this building required a code to gain access.

James turned on the lights, and Mak took in the lush surroundings—the Thomas brothers didn't do things by halves. Thick, red drapes covered every wall and the floor was covered in a soft, long-pile carpet that looked expensive. Twelve, wide velvet chairs were lined up in three rows.

"Very nice indeed," Mak said as James pressed a button that activated the drapes at the front of the room, revealing a screen that took up the entire wall.

"Thank you," James said, smiling as he walked toward a mahogany bar. He opened a cupboard to reveal a refrigerator. "What would you like to drink?" he asked, stepping aside so she could see the selection.

There was a range of juices and soft drinks, but Mak chose water. James retrieved two bottles and closed the refrigerator.

"Popcorn?"

Mak didn't really think she could stomach much, but James looked excited by the red-and-white striped machine that sat atop the bar. Mak moved forward to take a closer look. "Where did you get this?"

James chuckled. "To be honest, I'm not sure—Deacon bought it somewhere. But we all love it."

"Popcorn it is," Mak said.

The machine lit up when James turned it on. From a jar next to the machine, James scooped some kernels and tipped them into a slot in the side of the machine.

"Now we wait," he said.

"How often do you use this room?" Mak asked, trying to get a more accurate picture of what his life was like.

"Not enough, actually. We all work a lot, but it's a nice luxury to have when we need some downtime away from the world. Sometimes we do movie marathons in here, which are fun, but it doesn't happen often."

The kernels started popping and rebounding off the glass walls of the machine.

James opened up a drawer and pulled out a remote. He turned on the screen, bringing up a menu, and then threw it to her. She caught it with one hand.

"Good reflexes," he said with a hint of applaud.

Mak scrolled through the movie selection as James returned his attention to the popcorn.

"What kind of movies do you like to watch?" Mak asked.

"Anything except chick flick movies. Please don't make me watch one of those," James said with pleading eyes.

Mak grinned; she didn't like them either. She selected a new thriller and once the popcorn was done, James tipped it into a large bowl, salted it, and held out the bowl for her.

She popped a piece in her mouth. "Delicious."

James winked and, carrying the popcorn and water, led them to the two seats in the center of the first row.

Mak sank down into the chair. They were so comfortable, better than any other cinema chair she'd sat in.

"You can use these buttons to recline them," James said, pressing on the buttons controlling his chair. He relaxed into a half-upright position. Mak kicked off her shoes and reclined her chair back, pulling her knees up to her chest.

James pulled his phone from his pocket, pressed a few buttons on an app, and then the room went dark, lit only by the large screen.

James shifted in his chair, and Mak felt that same sensation she had at the construction site. Everything felt heightened in the dark. He leaned over, cupping her cheek with one hand. Mak's chest tightened as their lips touched and his tongue stroked hers. The man might not date, but he certainly knew how to kiss.

He pulled back but held her hand, resting it in his lap.

The movie started and they didn't speak again, nor did James make another move, but he did continue to hold her hand, his fingers stroking over her knuckles every now and then.

Mak lost track of the time, her mind distracted by either the trial or the man next to her, and when the movie credits rolled she was surprised the movie was over already.

James adjusted the lighting again, creating a soft, dim atmosphere. He rolled onto his side, and a faint line glistened along the edge of his jaw. A scar. Mak wondered how he got it, and if she even wanted to know.

Mak held her breath as he leaned in and brought their lips together. She felt a rush of energy flood her body as she kissed him back. His body was warm, almost hot, and it felt comforting. Everything about him felt right—the way he kissed her and the way he held her.

He sucked on her lower lip, and she moaned softly.

He dipped his tongue in her mouth, and she kissed him back.

"We should go upstairs," James said with a husky voice.

Mak looked into his eyes and nodded her head. Her brain knew it was the right thing to do, but her libido was having trouble understanding. "We should," she said unconvincingly.

James bit his lip and his eyes lingered on her, and then he put his chair back into the upright position. He stood up, waiting at the foot of her chair as it moved back into its original position. He held out his hand for her, helping her out of the chair. He picked up the half-empty bowl of popcorn and placed it by the machine, along with their empty water bottles.

"A maid will wash it in the morning," he said by way of explanation.

James turned off the lights, and they walked back to the elevator. The building was silent; they hadn't encountered another person all night.

James pressed one button on the elevator panel, and a few seconds later they arrived at her floor. James unlocked her apartment, which he always seemed to do for her, and closed the door behind him—but Mak knew he wasn't staying the night.

"Thank you for tonight," she said. It really was nice to have company, and Mak wondered if James, too, got tired of being alone.

"Thank you," he said quietly, tilting her chin up. He placed a sweet, innocent kiss on her lips and then exhaled a deep breath. "Good night, Mak."

~

The call came in at eleven in the morning: the jury had reached a verdict on all three counts.

Mak stood in the courtroom with squared shoulders and a stony face. It was the moment of truth.

"Ladies and gentlemen, I understand you have reached a verdict on all three counts."

"We have, Your Honor."

"In the case of Jodi Nelson, on the charge of murder in the first degree, how do you find?"

"We find the defendant guilty."

Mak's heart fluttered with a whisper of relief. *One down.*

"In the case of Ashleigh Brown, on the charge of murder in the first degree, how do you find?"

"We find the defendant guilty."

Two down.

"In the case of Kate Loren, on the charge of murder in the first degree, how do you find?"

"We find the defendant not guilty."

Two out of three—it wasn't good enough.

Mak looked down at the desk, knowing she now had to face the families. Two would be pleased, one would be disappointed.

She picked up her satchel and walked to the benches where they were sitting.

She greeted Jodie's parents first, and then Ashleigh's. And then she moved to Kate's parents.

Kate's mother looked at her through glistening eyes and Mak's heart wrenched.

"I'm sorry," Mak said.

Kate's mother shook her head. "Don't apologize to us. No one could've done better, Makaela," she said. Mak had told her many times to call her Mak, but she said she preferred Makaela because it sounded sweeter—which was the exact reason Mak didn't like it. "That man is going to prison, regardless of Kate's verdict, and that's enough for us. She would be happy with that. Thank you for fighting for her, and for the other women."

Mak squeezed her hands. "Thank you," she said.

"How long will he go away for?" Kate's father asked.

"I don't know; that will be determined by the judge. At the minimum he will serve two life sentences of twenty to twenty-five years. Given his age, that means he will spend every remaining hour of his life in prison."

"That's all we ever wanted," he said as a tear ran down his cheek. "If he's in prison, he can't hurt anyone else—that's the most important thing."

Mak simply nodded her head.

Mak wanted to fight it, to appeal the verdict, but if Kate's family didn't want to go down that road, she wouldn't. She would do what was best for the family because that was her obligation—not her own career satisfaction.

Mak said goodbye, spotting Cami who was waiting for her.

"Congratulations," she said, sporting a huge grin and sparkling eyes.

"Thanks," Mak said, mustering the smile she knew was appropriate but didn't feel in that moment. *Two out of three.*

Cami gave her an analyzing look, softly shaking her head, and said, "You're a hard woman to please. You should be happy."

"Can we go? I'd like to get through the media and back to my office," Mak said. She wanted to be alone.

As they walked, Mak noticed Cami seemed to be particularly close today. "What's up? You're invading my personal space."

Cami chuckled. "I've got strict instructions to be extra diligent today. James increased your security again last night, which seems a little over cautious, but he's been in a rather good mood these past few days—which is interesting—so I'm just keeping my mouth shut and following orders."

She knows, Mak figured by the way Cami looked at her. But how did she know?

A reporter stepped out in front of Mak as they exited the courthouse.

"Mrs. Ashwood, what about Kate Loren's verdict? Will you keep fighting for her?"

"That's yet to be determined," Mak said politely but firmly as she continued to walk. The reporters were yelling questions so loudly that Mak had trouble hearing the actual questions. She answered a few more and then Cami escorted her down to the car.

"Jesus," Mak said, exhaling as the car doors closed and they drove off. "That was insane."

"Did you hear that reporter?" Cami asked, laughing. "He said they're calling you the angel with horns."

"That's ridiculous," Mak said.

"I don't know, I think it's quite appropriate. You look like an angel, but you sure don't act like one." Cami looked behind them and Mak copied her, kneeling on the seat to look out the rear window.

Cami quickly put a hand on her shoulder, pushing her down. "Don't do that, you might get shot."

"So might you," Mak rebutted.

"Copy," Cami said. And then looked at Mak, "See, you just got me in trouble. James said to keep your head down."

Mak sighed, sliding down against the leather chair.

Two out of three. Damn.

Mak tried to push the disappointment aside, the feeling that she let Kate's family down, but she couldn't, and she knew it would take some time to let this trial go. She'd known the risks, and she'd known Kate's case in particular was going to be tough, and this was just part of the job. In theory, in her head, she knew she should be ecstatic. Two guilty verdicts. But her heart had yet to catch up with her mind.

They pulled up into a foreign parking lot and Mak looked around. Where were they?

Cami grabbed her bag and basically hauled her out and into the car that had pulled up beside them. Mak was in the back seat and the car was moving before she realized she'd changed cars.

"What the hell?" Mak muttered.

"Just a precaution."

Mak knew it was James's voice before she realized he was in the front passenger seat. She looked at the driver: Deacon. And Cami sat next to her.

"Well done, Mak, well done," Deacon said once they were back on the road.

"Yeah," Mak said noncommittally.

James turned in his seat, sticking his head between the headrest and the door. Only she could see his face. "Congratulations, Mak," he said. It wasn't his words but the intensity of his eyes. She could see there was so much more he wanted to say, and she also knew he knew what she was thinking. *I wasn't good enough.*

"Do you wish you could go for the death penalty for this bastard?" Deacon asked.

"I don't believe in the death penalty. I don't believe we get to make that decision . . . to decide who lives or dies," Mak said, crossing her legs.

"So who does get to decide?" Deacon asked.

"Whichever God you believe in, I suppose," Mak said. "But I will push for two life sentences. He should never have the privilege of being a free man ever again."

"Mmm," Deacon said.

"But he decided to take the lives of three women, and I'm sure many more, so why not just kill him?" James asked casually. "God didn't decide the fate of those women, he did, so why should God get a say in when he dies?" It wasn't a debate, but rather a question out of interest.

"But if we kill him, aren't we just as bad?" Mak responded.

"No. He deserves to die, they didn't—that's the difference," James said.

"I don't think it's our decision to make," Mak said again. "And in fact I've never agreed with it. There is no evidence to confirm the death penalty deters criminals from committing crimes that carry the punishment, innocent men and women are unfortunately convicted all too often, and morally I don't agree with the government taking a life."

"Fair enough," James said, and then all was quiet again and Deacon looked sideways at his brother. Mak wondered what that look was for but she knew if she asked she'd be given an evasive answer.

Back in her office, Mak sat quietly, contemplating the case and last night with James. And then their conversation in the car. Some of their views, particularly those attaining to the law, were very different. But even on those, they seemed to be able to respectfully disagree.

Mak looked at the ring on her right finger, the wedding band she still felt obligated to wear, although she rarely thought of him. But something had shifted in her, and she no longer wanted to wear it. *I made a mistake.* Mak allowed herself to finally admit the truth. It was young love, and they should never have gotten married. She took one last look at it, slipped it off her finger, and put it in her desk drawer. That chapter of her life was closed.

Mak picked up her phone and looked through the tens of congratulatory messages coming in. She paused on Maya's, mostly because she liked the first word: *Drinks??*

Yes, that's exactly what I need.

She called Maya.

"My superstar sister!" Maya said, greeting her. "So, how pissed off are you about the third verdict?"

Maya knew her better than anyone.

"Not happy," Mak responded.

"I figured as much. You are way too hard on yourself. I'm proud of you, and Mom and Dad are already toasting to their mega-successful daughter. You should enjoy this, Mak, enjoy the moment."

"Yeah, yeah," Mak said. She knew what she should do, she just didn't know how to do it.

"So, are we going out for a drink?" Maya asked.

"Please. Some of the team here are going to that bar on the corner, Siglo. I said I would join them so why don't you meet me there at seven?"

"Sounds good."

"Great, I'll see you soon," Mak said, hanging up the phone.

19

JAMES THOMAS

The bar was busy, and it was easy to be a nameless face in the crowd. James, Deacon, and Tom sat together on a couch no more than fifteen feet from Mak, drinking their sodas.

James knew she was upset about the verdict, which was unreasonable, yet he got it. She had very high expectations for herself, which was both a blessing and a curse. It was what drove her to be successful, but then she was never satisfied.

He watched her covertly, his eyes seemingly never leaving her, nor did they linger. His body yearned for her, and it had since he'd said goodbye to her last night—it was no doubt a result of the unreleased desire.

Maya ordered another round of drinks, and James mulled over his next move. Now that her trial was over, he wanted to talk to her. He wondered if he should wait, given how disappointed she seemed with the verdict. But that wasn't a feeling that was going to go away overnight—it would take considerable time. And he wanted Mak to hear his security requirements because if she didn't like them, which he expected, it was better to end this sooner rather than later.

"I'm going to do a sweep," James said, standing with his drink. The men nodded their heads, unfazed—it wasn't out of protocol.

When he was out of Deacon's sight, he typed a text message to Mak:

If you want to talk tonight, perhaps don't have another drink. We can't discuss anything if you're not sober.

James sent the message and then continued his sweep.

Mak had been on her phone all night, replying to messages and phone calls, so Deacon would think nothing of it when she checked her phone again. Deacon was a problem he was going to have to deal with soon, if they did decide to take things further.

James saw nothing alarming as he walked through the bar. He checked his phone, but there was no response from Mak. He went back to the couch.

Over the next thirty minutes he watched the glass in front of her—she didn't take a mouthful, but she also hadn't replied to his message. Mak didn't like being told what to do—which is why he'd worded the message the way he had—but even still, she had to be defiant. If they did go down this path, they were going to butt heads constantly. James just hoped the make-up sex was going to be good.

"Exit." James heard Cami's voice through his earpiece.

Finally.

Deacon got up and went to get the car while James and his men prepared to escort Mak out. Mak said her goodbyes, and then Cami gave the code to move.

They formed two unified lines as Mak walked down the middle and into the car. He climbed into the passenger seat, while the other men loaded into the cars in front and behind them. James wasn't taking any chances tonight.

They detoured several times until they reached Thomas Security. Cami took Mak upstairs, while James and Deacon went to Samuel's office. Thankfully there was nothing to debrief, so it was a quick catch-up. Deacon was heading out again tonight, to cover security for another client, which was perfectly convenient. As was the fact that he'd gone to bed early last night with a headache.

James excused himself and made his way to Mak's apartment.

He let himself in, and she smiled as she looked up from her phone.

He found himself excited, even a little nervous.

"Thank you for the message . . . much appreciated," Mak said, tilting her head to the side. James would've thought she was mad except for the smile on her lips.

"You didn't respond," James said, feigning insult.

He cupped her small face in his hands, eager to taste her lips. His body felt heavy with arousal and anticipation.

She tilted her chin up and their lips brushed. He closed his eyes, enjoying the kiss, memorizing it because he wasn't sure how many more he would get.

"How are you feeling?" James asked.

She ran her fingers through her long hair. "Fine. Are we going to talk now that my trial is over?"

"If you're up for it. I really enjoy spending time with you, but there's not much point if you don't think you'll be able to live with the type of security I would want to put in place. And that's okay, I would understand that. But the sooner you hear it, the better, I think."

Mak nodded her head thoughtfully.

"Come upstairs," he said, taking her hand.

They took the stairs, as usual, because it was faster than waiting for the elevator, and he sat her on the kitchen island.

"You haven't eaten since yesterday—smoothies don't count—so I'll cook something quick and—"

"You can cook?"

"I'm no master chef, but yes I can cook," James said. "Cooking is a survival skill."

Mak barked out a laugh. "In this century? Okay, Indiana Jones."

"Okay, smart-ass," James said, leaning on the island bench-top so they were eye level. "Here's a test. You're in Boston, and someone is following you. You manage to get away from them, and find a vacant apartment to hide in for a few days, but you need to eat. You can't use a credit card because they might track it, so what are you going to do?"

"Go to the supermarket and pay cash?"

"What kind of supermarket?"

"The closest one," Mak suggested.

"No, you go to the smallest one, the mom-and-pop one, the one without security cameras." James grinned. "Now, what are you going to buy at the supermarket that doesn't involve cooking?"

Mak was quick with her answers. "Cereal and a carton of milk. Or a frozen dinner."

"Cereal has little nutritional value and it's loaded with sugar, which will give you a rush, followed by a crash. Too much dairy can also make your body sluggish. And, unfortunately, at the mom-and-pop store you're probably not going to have a huge range of frozen meal choices, so chances are they won't be high in protein or energy. Now, two weeks later, they've found you again. You try and run but you're too tired and you're not fast enough. What happens then?"

"They catch me?" Mak guessed.

"And then what happens?"

Mak rolled her eyes. "Then, James, I wait for my Prince Charming, you, to come and rescue me."

"Prince Charming might come too late, and your fairy tale won't have a happy ending," he said seriously. "So, if we're going to date, you're going to have to learn to cook. You're also going to have to learn how and what to eat in the wild, but we can work up to that."

Mak groaned. "If this is normally your approach to seducing women, I now understand why you're single."

James laughed. "Oh no, this is not normal, this is all just for you."

"Just to clarify, where and how do you think I would end up in the wild with the need to hunt and gather?"

"Impossible to say at this stage, but anything could happen—you wouldn't believe the places I've ended up stranded in. Once, on what I thought would be a routine trip to Tokyo, we had to take a detour and then ended up stuck in a forest for ten days. Anything is possible where I'm concerned," James said. *An unexpected detour that was definitely Kyoji Tohmatsu's fault.* "Omelet?"

"Please," Mak said. "So, what else, as your potential girlfriend, would I have to agree to?"

He pulled the omelet ingredients from the fridge and gathered a knife and chopping board and placed it all on the bench in front of Mak.

"You will need to be able to protect yourself, so you will need to be physically fit and acquire a few new skills," James said, chopping the onion.

"Such as?"

"Such as working out in the gym for an hour every day, and then doing an hour of weapons training. Given your size, learning how to shoot a gun will be your priority."

"Two hours every day?" Mak asked.

"Yes," James responded as he chopped the rest of the omelet ingredients. He knew this wasn't going to be an easy sell.

"I'm not applying to be a bodyguard," Mak said. "I'm supposed to have bodyguards protect me. Absolutely not, I don't have time for that—particularly when I have a big trial on."

"You make time," James said. "Cami does it, even with the hours you spend with her."

"It's Cami's job, it's not mine," Mak said. "How about half an hour of each, an hour in total?"

"It's not negotiable, Mak," James said.

"Everything is negotiable. Or, what if I agree to it, but during a trial I would get a pass for at least some of the days?"

"How many of the days?" James said with a smirk.

"All of the days," Mak suggested guiltily.

James shook his head. "No. How long do your trials usually last?"

"Mmm, somewhere between a couple weeks and a couple months."

James mixed the ingredients in the bowl and then cracked the eggs. "This is my offer, and it's a huge compromise, so you should take it," he said. "During the trial you can get a pass, for all of the days, but you make up every single hour in the days after the trial."

"I'll make up one of those hours if you train me," she said, biting her lip.

"I'm not sure how productive that will be," James said, his eyes lingering on her lips.

"That's my final offer," she said, shrugging her shoulders.

"Fine," James said, thinking that if he offered to train her for those make-up sessions he could entice her into the gym for a few additional hours. "Next, I'm serious about you learning to cook. But I will teach you that, and you will enjoy it," he said, winking at her.

"I accept," Mak said, grinning.

"Next, if you needed to travel within the United States, Cami would go with you, and preferably I would too, depending on the situation. If you need to go overseas, you wouldn't be able to go unless I go with you."

"What?" Mak said, the playfulness disappearing. "I'm planning to meet Maya in Spain in a few months."

"This one is definitely not negotiable, Mak. I would have to go with you, or you couldn't go. That's a risk I'm not prepared to take."

"Why is overseas more of a threat? It's not like I'm going to go to Syria," Mak said.

Because I have more enemies overseas than you can imagine. "Do you agree or not?"

"No, I'm not agreeing." She was adamant, and James's heart felt heavier than he thought it would.

He put the knife down and frowned. "This isn't negotiable, Mak. I told you that you wouldn't like the security requirements, and this is one of the most important ones. If you can't agree, there's really no point in discussing anything further," James said, pressing his lips together.

Mak eyed him, not reacting at all. Several moments passed. "What are the other requirements?"

"It doesn't matter what the others are, since you have to agree to all of them," James responded.

"Well, I'll consider that one while you talk about the others," she said.

James thought it over. It seemed pointless to continue, but he supposed if she could live with the other requirements, in time, with a miracle, she might come to accept the travel arrangement.

James walked over to the stovetop and warmed up a pan. He added just enough oil so it wouldn't stick and poured in the mix. "You would have a driver at all times, a minimum of two bodyguards at all times, cameras in your apartment. Which, speaking of, I have found one for you. It's in a very good building and it's not far from here."

"When can I see it?"

"This weekend, if you'd like. Or any time next week. I would prefer you stay here at Thomas Security, though, until we work out exactly who is behind the notes and recent events," he said, sliding a white envelope that had been sitting behind the fruit bowl in her direction. "This is the apartment. We refer a lot of clients to this developer, so we get a subsidized rate. Take a look...if you don't like it, I'll find something else."

Mak opened the envelope and looked at the images and the floor plan. "This is a very expensive apartment. I can't afford this even with the subsidy, I'm sure."

"If you can afford the apartment you were in before, then you can afford this one. We give them a lot of business, Mak, and I don't normally negotiate such a substantial subsidy, so they kindly did this for us," James said, checking his omelet—it was nearly done.

"And while we're on the subject of money," James continued, "I would cover the costs of your security. You can't afford this level of security long-term, and you would need it because of me, and therefore I should pay for it."

Mak narrowed her eyes. "How do you know I can't afford it?"

"Unless you have millions stashed away somewhere, or your name is Jayce Tohmatsu, you can't afford it," James said, watching her carefully. He had no intention of telling her about the double life her husband had led, nor the money she could claim.

"Unfortunately, I have not, and I am not," she said, resting her elbows on the counter and folding her hands beneath her chin.

James didn't think she knew about the offshore accounts; at least he knew for sure now.

He lifted the omelet out and sliced it in two. He plated each serving, retrieved some cutlery, and put it down in front of her, remaining on the opposite side of the island.

"Would you agree to me footing your security bill?" James asked, noticing she was listening but not actually agreeing to much.

She took a bite of the omelet, letting the fork linger between her lips.

James loved it, but he wasn't going to let her distract him. "Yes or no, Mak?"

"I'll have to consider it," she said casually.

"Yes or no?" James pressed.

"Can you afford it? Is your name Jayce Tohmatsu?"

Mak took another bite, and James was glad she was at least eating.

"My name is not Jayce Tohmatsu, but I assure you I can afford it. Yes or no, and stop stalling."

"Okay, then, but I still haven't seen a bill for your damages thus far. Where is it?"

"I don't know. I'll have to check with accounts—I'll follow it up on Monday morning." Her bill didn't exist, he'd already made sure of it, but he hadn't quite worked out how to sell that to her yet.

"Thank you. This omelet is very good," Mak said, taking another bite.

"You're welcome. What do you think about the apartment?" he said, not letting her sidetrack him.

"What's not to like?" she said. "Is this your apartment of choice, though? I really don't want to move again."

"It's the best building for you to be in, other than this one, so you wouldn't need to move again. I promise."

"Good. Anything else?"

"No, but you haven't agreed to the travel requirement, so the ball's in your court."

She put her fork down. "I don't know how I can agree to that."

"I get that, but I can't offer you anything else. I'm not prepared to do this by halves, Mak—I don't normally take risks with any of my clients, and that's why this business is as successful as it is. And when it comes to you, you'd better believe I will be even more cautious. Having a girlfriend at all is a huge risk, and I have to try and minimize that with more extreme measures—not imposing this level of security would just be stupidity on my behalf.

"I wish it wasn't this way, but it's the only way it can be. I understand if you want to walk away, in fact I encourage you to. My life comes with a ton of baggage and risks and worry that you shouldn't have to concern yourself with."

James could see the mental war raging in her eyes.

"Can I think about it?" Mak finally asked.

"Of course you can—for as long you need," he said, looking straight into her eyes. He wouldn't force her to make a decision until she was ready to, especially not one she might soon come to regret.

She gave him a small smile.

James felt his phone vibrate in his pocket: *Deacon Thomas.*

James didn't know why he was calling, but he wasn't expecting the news to be good.

20

MAK ASHWOOD

Mak ate the remainder of her omelet but her attention was on James. She'd noticed his telephone conversations were almost always a combination of one-syllable words: yes, or no, or fine. Every now and then he strung a sentence together, giving away the only clues to the conversation.

"Ah, I'm not sure. I'll have to check with Cami to see what she has planned. I'll give her a call and get back to you," James said, and then hung up and put his phone on the bench top.

"What are your plans this weekend?" he asked her.

"Me?" Mak asked, surprised.

"Yes, you. The client Deacon is with wants to go for an unscheduled trip this weekend, and wants Deacon to accompany him. But depending on what you're doing, I might need him here."

Did both James and Deacon watch her all the time?

"I haven't gotten that far. Given the trial is over, I just want to relax, go to barre . . . have a quiet weekend."

"If I tell Deacon to go, you have to have a very quiet weekend," James said.

"How do you define a very quiet weekend? I'm starting to think I need a *Terms and Conditions* document to go with your requirements."

James gave her that sexy smirk that she loved. "It means that you stay in this building for majority of the weekend."

She brought the tip of her thumb to her lips, thinking it over. What was she going to do in this building all weekend? "Well, that depends. While I think over this travel requirement, are we going to spend time together?"

He didn't answer her immediately, and she knew what he was thinking: there's no point getting to know each other if it wasn't going anywhere. But at the same time, she wasn't going to sit in her apartment all weekend with nothing to do but roam the Internet. If she wasn't going to be with him, she was definitely going out.

"For this weekend, yes," he said finally.

Mak nodded her head. "Tell him to go, then."

James brought the phone back to his ear, holding it in place with his shoulder while he loaded their plates and cutlery into the dishwasher.

Mak listened as he told Deacon she was more or less staying in for the weekend. She noted he didn't say he'd spoken with Cami, or that he'd spoken with Mak—he omitted that part of the conversation completely, leaving Deacon to assume the route he'd taken. *Crafty move, Thomas.*

"Why are you looking at me like that?" James asked with an odd expression on his face.

Mak shrugged her shoulders, playing dumb. "Like what?" She knew with a man like James it was best if he didn't know what she was thinking—the more she could put together about him, without him realizing, the better. There was a lot you could learn about a person via keen observation.

He tilted his head to the side, studying her now. She gave him nothing, and then, when he'd obviously given up, he walked around the island and sat down on the bench seat next to her, his legs forming a *V* around her.

"Are you tired?" James asked.

Mak looked at the time on the oven clock, seeing it was well after midnight. She was exhausted after the week she'd had but she wasn't quite ready to say goodnight either.

"Not particularly," she said.

"You're a good liar," he whispered as he leaned in to kiss her.

She brushed her lips over his and felt her chest flower with lust. She closed her eyes and kissed him. He moaned and then dragged her stool closer. He took control of the kiss, exploring her mouth with his fluid tongue. When he said her name, it sounded equal parts lust and torture.

"I'm finding it very difficult to get to know you without ripping your clothes off," James said.

Mak chuckled. "We can just make out like teenagers do," she said, her tongue peeking out between her lips.

His eyes dropped to her lips, and he stood up, holding out his hand. He led her to the couch in the living room and wrapped his arms around her waist. He thrust his tongue into her mouth and lowered their bodies onto the couch, holding her in one arm and steadying himself with the other. He did it so effortlessly, so seamlessly, that before she knew it she was beneath him, her head resting on the cushion.

The weight of his body on top of her fueled her arousal, and she felt her cheeks flush. He kissed the hollow behind her ear and she closed her eyes, enjoying the moment.

All Mak had to do was agree to the one last requirement, but she felt like she was betraying herself and giving up her independence. What woman couldn't go away with her family, or on a girls' weekend without her boyfriend coming along? What girl had cameras in her house, bodyguards, and her boyfriend and his brother following her every move? A girl who dated James Thomas, that's who.

"I'm never going to ask you to say yes, Mak," James whispered. "I'm never going to beg you to give up so much just to be with me. I won't do that."

She respected him for that, but with a mind clouded by arousal she wished he would ask her.

"I know," Mak said with resignation. She adjusted the cushion beneath her head so that they could talk. "I would be able to go away whenever I want, though, right? I just have to have you with me if it's international."

He thought it through before he answered. "As long as I can go with you, yes. But there are some countries that are completely off limits, and I don't want you to go there at all."

Mak raised her eyebrows—she knew she needed a fine-print document. "Such as?"

"I would prefer not to say at this stage," he said with a straight face. "But I wouldn't imagine they are countries you'd be intending to visit anyway, so I don't see it being an issue."

"I think perhaps you should say," Mak said.

James sighed. "Well, to begin with, any country that is in war is completely off limits. And then Belarus, Lithuania . . . and neighboring countries would also not be a good idea." James rolled onto his side, squeezing between her and the cushions, and rested up on his elbow.

Mak needed to brush up on her geography skills, but she couldn't foresee wanting to visit any such countries.

She searched her mind for an alternative, a compromise that would make this requirement bearable. "So, if you can travel with me, and it's to a country you approve of, then we could go on a group trip, right?"

His eyebrows threaded together. "A group trip?"

"Yes. Like a couple's trip? We could go with Maya and her fiancé, and even Zahra and Jayce. Jayce travels with security anyway, right?"

He looked bemused.

"What?" Mak asked.

He shook his head, smiling. "I've never done a couple's trip in my life. And not once while I was working with Jayce did I think that in the future we might end up holidaying together with our girlfriends," he said, laughing.

"You've got to get out more, James," Mak joked.

"Yes, we could do couple's trips. But we stay in the hotel of my choice, and we fly private."

"Fly private? Perhaps you are Jayce Tohmatsu," Mak said, laughing softly.

James grinned. "Actually, Jayce rarely uses their jet unless there is a group on board—he's quite a conservative spender, given his wealth. I'm sure he'll use it more now that he has Zahra, though. But I'm not concerned with the luxuries of it as much as the security benefits. It's logistically much easier, and it makes it less likely for anyone to track our movements."

"I see," Mak said. It was an alternative, a very enticing one, but it was still a compromise on her independence.

"I don't want you to make a decision tonight. It's not a choice you should make lightly," James said, squeezing her hand. His fingers brushed over her bare right ring finger and this time she could read his thoughts.

"I took it off," Mak said.

"I noticed . . . while you were having drinks. Is that ring your wedding band?"

"It is," Mak said, quietly. "Does it bother you that I wear it—wore it?" Mak corrected herself. She had no intention of wearing it again.

"Maybe it should but it doesn't," he said casually. "To be honest, I just don't think of you as a married woman. Perhaps because I never knew you back then."

"I started wearing my wedding band on my right hand a little while after Eric went missing, mostly just to avoid the questions that came with having a husband who disappeared. It generates some uncomfortable conversations," Mak said. "I think from there I wore it out of obligation, maybe trying to convince myself I was a good wife when I had never been."

It was easy to be open with James, despite the world of secrets that lived between them. He never seemed to judge her, he just listened, and there was something very beautiful about that.

"Anyway," Mak said, "that chapter is well and truly closed now."

"Do you want to get married again? Do you want a family?" James asked.

She'd given a lot of consideration to both of those questions. "I don't need to get married again. It's not that I don't believe in commitment, but I don't think you need a certificate to prove it. Children . . . I don't know. I really can't imagine myself as a mother. I can't imagine going to the playground and doing all of those kinds of things. I just want to work—I want to be a good lawyer, and that's how I want to spend my time. Is that a bad thing? Does that make me selfish?"

James gently cupped her cheek, turning her face to him. He leaned forward to place a gentle kiss on her lips. "No, it doesn't. You don't have to want children, and there's nothing wrong with you if you don't."

"Do you want to get married? Do you want children?" Mak reciprocated the questions.

He relaxed his arm over her stomach, letting it rest there. "I'd never thought marriage was an option—I'm still barely convinced having a girlfriend is an option. Marriage might be doable, but children . . . I don't want to have children, Mak. You can make a choice to be part of my life or not, with the information that I can give you. But children are innocent and they can't make the kind of choice you're making. I don't want to bring a child into my world."

"Okay," Mak said. Not having children wasn't a big deal to her, and in some way it was a relief to hear he would never ask her for it— a further confirmation motherhood was not her thing.

"While we're on this subject . . . I know that you're on the pill—we have a list of medications for all of our clients—but if we end up going further I will always wear a condom. The pill isn't one hundred percent effective, or you could accidentally forget to take it. It's just a risk I won't take."

He looked like he was expecting some kind of reaction from her. She thought it was a little over-precautious, but otherwise it didn't particularly worry her.

"What if I were to get an IUD? Would that make it easier? It would eliminate the risk of me forgetting to take it," Mak said.

"They're still not one hundred percent effective. I could at some stage get a vasectomy, but the recovery period, however minor, concerns me given my lifestyle and the fact that things can potentially erupt at any moment, for any of our clients."

Mak nodded her head.

It would mean that he would never get to truly feel her, though, and vice-versa. "Not even once, just to feel things properly?"

James didn't look offended, or agitated, or anything else. He was his signature calm. He simply shook his head.

"Okay, if that makes you feel better, that's fine," Mak said.

James rolled back on top of her, and Mak wrapped her arms around his back, feeling his muscles flex with just the slightest movement.

She felt the heaviness pooling in her pelvis as he sucked on her neck again. Mak closed her eyes, drowning in the sensation. She couldn't stand the teasing, but she didn't want him to stop, either.

James groaned and pulled back. "In so many ways we are perfect for each other, and in so many ways we're so wrong. Or I'm so wrong for you, to be correct. I've made peace with my past and most of the things I've done, but I never knew how much it would impact my future. My past is, and always will be, a wedge between us and there is nothing I can do to make it any better."

"If not for your past, we may never have met," Mak said, stroking his head.

"Maybe not. Or maybe. Life is the master of organization, and it always gets what it wants."

"Do you think we would've ended up meeting, regardless?"

"I think it's possible. Maybe life is using my past to punish me now. It would be fair, if that's what's happening," James said.

"Do you think you're a bad person?"

"No. I've done some bad things, but I don't think I'm a bad person. And I can't change the past now, so I don't see any point in living in regret."

Mak considered it. "I don't think there is any point."

James slid one leg between hers. He looked into her eyes, and she leaned in to kiss his lips. He opened his mouth, thrusting his tongue in. She felt that pooling sensation in her hips again and she wanted more, but she knew she wasn't going to get it.

"Out of all the potential problems we might have, I don't think the sex is going to be one of them," James said with a voice like gravel.

Mak smiled as she rolled on to her side, facing him. Their bodies were flush, and she kissed his chest. She loved the smell of his cologne as she inhaled deeply.

He ran his fingers through her hair and kissed the crown of her head.

We could be so good together. But there were so many obstacles in their path.

Mak closed her eyes. She felt her body relax, warm and cozy. It was late, and she'd just lived the most intense week of her life, but in the security of his arms it was easy to drift to sleep.

21

JAMES THOMAS

She slept with the peacefulness of an innocent child. No tension in her face, no tremors in her body.

James lay on the couch, looking at the women in his arms. How many more nights was he going to get to do this? How long before he would have to let her go? There was a chance, a slim chance, that she would agree to his requirements, but that meant she had to give up a lot. She was a grown, successful woman, and she should be able to do whatever she wanted. But if she wanted him, she had to give up some of her independence. And for Mak Ashwood that was going to be a hard task.

He grabbed the afghan from the back of the couch and draped it over them. James closed his eyes but he didn't want to sleep. That foreboding feeling of uncertainty, that something was wrong, was back. He'd felt it earlier today, and the unease gripped him again now that he had a clear head. He didn't want to think it, but something told him they weren't going to get many more nights like this.

At some point James must have dozed off because his phone woke him. He looked at the time—unbelievably, it was after ten in the morning. His body-clock had completely failed him. Or, perhaps, it knew to make the most of the calm night.

"Cami," James whispered. He knew where this call was going.

"Why are you whispering, James?"

"She's with me," James said.

Cami had made several observations over the past few days, and James thought it would come as no surprise that Mak was with him.

"Yes, I thought she must be. I was going to see if she wanted coffee. Does Deacon know about this?"

"Hang on," James said, trying to disentangle himself without waking up Mak. He kept Cami waiting until he was in his bedroom. "No, he doesn't. I'm giving Mak the choice, with a list of requirements she has to agree to. If she decides that this is what she wants and things move forward, I will tell him. But right now, other than her sleeping on my couch, and that is literally all that's going on, I have little to tell Deacon that he doesn't already know."

Cami whistled. "It's going to be your funeral."

"No, it's my life, and he will have to come to accept it," James said. "Anyway, can you be nice and bring us coffee?"

"I'm always nice. Look, I don't think what you're doing is a brilliant idea, and even you know it's not, but if you decide to do this you know that I'll support you and help you protect her."

James smiled. They were a dysfunctional family, but they were always there for each other. "Thank you, and I mean that, Cami."

"Yeah, yeah, she's making you soft already."

James laughed. "Mission impossible. I'll wake her up now, so we'll see you soon."

"Catch ya," Cami said, ending the phone call.

James went into the kitchen, downed a glass of water, and went back into the living room. Mak was curled up in a tight ball and had her hands bundled under her chin, with a slight smile on her lips. She looked beautiful. He took one more lingering look before he attempted to wake her—it was quite a process.

"Mak."

"Mak."

"Mak, wake up," James said, shaking her shoulder now.

She opened her eyes, smiled, and then her eyes rolled back in her head.

James chuckled. "I've got coffee," he said.

"Coffee?" Her eyes opened again and then traveled around the room as if she forgot where she was.

"Well, Cami is actually the one bringing coffee, so I suggest you get up."

Mak scrunched up her nose. "You obviously told her I was here, right?"

"Yes, she knows," he said, kissing her lips.

Mak rubbed her eyes. "I need to shower and change my clothes."

"I need to jump in the shower too, and we've got time—she only just called. You can shower downstairs and then just come back up when you're done."

Mak simultaneously yawned and nodded her head. "What are we doing today?"

"Whatever you want. There are some other features of this building you might like. We have a swimming pool, a rooftop garden, a game room..."

Mak's eyes widened. "What kind of games do you have?"

"We have a pool table, arcade machines, Ping-Pong—"

"You have Ping-Pong?"

James beamed a grin. "We do. I take it you like the game?"

"We had one growing up, and I loved it. I should warn you, though, I'm very good." Mak nodded her head up and down, slowly and arrogantly.

"We'll see how good you are against the master," James said, smirking.

Mak scoffed. "I think you're overly confident."

James enjoyed her playfulness, and he enjoyed a competitive partner. He grabbed her as she stood up to leave. "You're going to lose," he whispered in her ear, but she pushed him away.

"We'll see," she said, smiling at him over her shoulder.

James watched her leave and then walked down the hallway to his bathroom. He took a quick shower and shaved before getting dressed. He went back to the kitchen and checked his email as he waited for either Cami or Mak to emerge. Cami appeared first.

She entered without knocking, as she always did, and carrying a holder with three coffees.

"Mornin'," she said, handing him a to-go cup. "Do you realize we have everything imaginable in this building but a decent coffee machine?"

"Well, we technically have one," James said with raised eyebrows.

"Yes, good ol' Deacon," Cami said.

Deacon had broken the coffee machine, knocking it off the counter while engaging in a testosterone-fueled play fight with one of their staff, so out of spite James refused to buy another one with company money. They broke enough things unintentionally; he didn't need careless staff to add to the damages bill—especially a co-owner as it set a bad example. Conveniently, Deacon rarely drank coffee, so he was in no hurry to go out and purchase a replacement. The rest of Thomas Security staff were getting very grumpy, though.

"I was looking at the expense report a few days ago. Do you know he's broken three cell phones this month?"

Cami held up her empty palms. "I still can't work out how that guy is so coordinated and yet manages to break so many things. Can you imagine what he was like as a child? He would've been destructive as fuck."

James laughed. He could imagine a little Deacon tearing up the house every time his parents turned their backs.

He heard a knock at his door and went to open it. Mak was dressed in ripped skinny jeans and a loose black sleeveless T-shirt that revealed just a slither of her toned abdomen. She looked good—very good. He placed a quick kiss on her cheek before he led her into the kitchen.

"Good morning," Mak said, greeting Cami with a sly grin.

Cami laughed. "I came with your favorite," she said, gesturing toward the lone coffee on the island bench.

Mak walked past James, without touching him, and took a seat beside Cami.

"What's the plan for today?" Cami asked.

"I'm going to beat James at Ping-Pong. Do you want to come and watch him lose?" Mak said with the widest smile James had ever seen on her face.

Cami threw her head back, laughing. And then she looked at James with dancing eyes. "Oh, Thomas, you've met your match," she said.

James chuckled. "You've yet to see my prowess, Mak."

"Just don't be a sore loser, James, no one likes them," Mak said smugly.

Cami laughed loudly again and James laughed too, despite the joke being on him.

"I do actually want to see this, but if you two are staying in, I'm going to take the day off. I need to catch up on some things while I can," Cami said.

While I can. Cami meant nothing by the words, he could tell by the tone of her voice, but something about that phrase filled him with apprehension. It made no sense whatsoever, but it added to the lingering fear he couldn't shake.

James knew he should take the opportunity to show Mak the apartment, but that innate sense that something was wrong was stopping him. He didn't want her to move out—she was safer here than anywhere.

"Take the day off, Cami, but don't go too far," James said, ruling out the chance of any apartment-viewing. *Don't go too far* was code for *don't leave this building.* She could do whatever she needed in her apartment, but he still wanted her close by.

"All right," she said, standing up. She drank the last of her coffee and put the cup in the kitchen trash. "Goodbye. And good luck today, Mak. I hope you crush him."

James glared at Cami, but she just laughed as she let herself out.

James took a seat next to Mak, and she cupped his face in her small hands. Her smooth skin felt good against his freshly-shaven face.

"Shall we eat? I'm hungry. But then I'm always hungry."

"Are you going to cook?"

"Yes. Eggs, pancakes, or oatmeal?"

She turned the decision over in her mind for a second. "Pancakes," she said, sealing her decision with a kiss.

James moaned, deepening what had started as an innocent kiss. His hand found the exposed skin of her waist. "I like this," he said with a gravelly voice.

"My top?" Mak asked between kisses.

"Mmm." His fingers brushed over her skin and her stomach contracted in response. "Pancake time," he said, forcing himself to pull away.

Mak watched him with heady eyes as he went to the refrigerator and pulled out the needed ingredients.

"Second cooking lesson in two days. So far so good," James said.

But Mak's attention for the cooking class quickly dissipated as her phone lit up on the bench. She ran her hand through her hair as she read the text. "I have to respond to a few messages from yesterday. And I still have to call my parents back."

James nodded. "Do it now while I cook," he said, letting her out of the cooking lesson—learning to cook pancakes wasn't really a survival skill.

She brought the phone to her ear as she walked out of the kitchen. He listened to her conversation as he cooked. Mak Ashwood put on a brave face, but he knew she was disappointed in the trial. Two out of three was not good enough for her.

She came back into the kitchen as he was flipping the last pancake.

"You haven't brought up the trial," he said casually, gauging her resistance to the conversation.

"What more is there to say?"

He fastened her hands behind his back. "That you won. That he will go to prison for the rest of his life. That you should be very proud. I know that you think you failed on some level, but you're very wrong."

"I know I should feel all of those things, but right now I'm one of those sore losers no one likes," she said, cracking a joke.

"I like them," James said, hugging her tight. He loved how she felt in his arms.

She didn't respond, but she didn't let go either. He let the pancake cook longer than it should have but didn't want to let her go.

"I can't cook, but I know that's going to burn," she said with a small smile.

James grinned. "I know." He turned the gas cooktop off and served the slightly over-browned pancake onto his plate.

They sat at the table and ate. James couldn't remember the last time he'd sat at the table, or if he ever had. They usually ate in Samuel's office.

"Is this how life will be?" Mak asked, cutting her pancake stack.

"What do you mean, exactly?"

"Will we spend most of our time hanging out together here?" Mak clarified.

"Not all of our time. Yes, I prefer to be here, because I don't have to look over my shoulder every second of the day. But we're also staying in today because right now you have an additional security threat that is not yet resolved. Once it is settled, we'll be able to do all of the normal things couples do—the only difference is there will be security following us. But that is what these guys are trained to do, Mak, and they're not actually watching us—they're watching everything around us. We're not a threat to ourselves, the threat is in the sideways peeks of a stranger on the street, or an unusual movement in a window. That's what they're looking for."

"Do you always have security following you?" Mak asked.

"Rarely, but if I'm going into a dangerous situation I would take someone like Deacon or Cami with me. I don't need additional security because I'm trained to watch everything around me and protect myself. It's a skill that developed over years, and now it's just ingrained in my psyche. I'm always watching everything—I can't help it anymore."

"Isn't that exhausting?"

"One would think so, but when you've done it most of your life, it's second nature."

Seemingly satisfied with his answers, Mak ate quietly for a minute.

"Oh, my gosh," she said, surprised. "I don't even know your age. How old are you?"

Her alarmed reaction was cute. "I'm thirty-eight," James said.

It was a lie he had to speak because he didn't know the answer to her question. The orphanage he'd grown up in didn't have a copy of his birth certificate, given that he'd been dumped on their doorstep as a small child, and Samuel hadn't been able to find one online either. James didn't know his parents' names, or the hospital he'd been born in, so he couldn't even try and find any medical records. With nothing else to go on, he'd done some biological testing. The precision of such tests had improved over the years, but the latest test still had an estimation accuracy give or take a couple of years. So based on all the facts he could piece together, thirty-eight years old was his best guess.

"I thought you were a few years younger," she said with a smile.

"It's my charming face," he joked.

Mak gave an exaggerated eye-roll. "Perhaps it's your enlarged ego."

James chuckled.

Mak pushed the plate away, indicating she was full. It was empty, and James was pleased to see she ate quite a bit for a woman her size. And if she agreed to his requirements and started training with Cami, she would need to eat every few hours to make sure she didn't lose any weight.

"So . . . I've been thinking about your requirements," Mak said, folding her hands onto the dining table like she was in a business meeting, "and I've come up with a few requirements of my own.

"I'm not yet agreeing to your travel requirements, but if I did, we would need to go on at least one vacation per year. And if my family plans a trip together, which they love to do, I will be going regardless of the location and hotel, and you will have to come and deal with it.

And believe me, you will regret it because, with six children, and their partners, it is absolute bedlam."

James smiled. He knew her family was unlikely to book a trip to Russia any time soon, so he could probably agree.

"Next," Mak continued, "you have to tell me more about your past. It doesn't have to be work-related things, but, for example, things like your age, which you just told me—there must be similar things about you that I can surely know without it being a security risk."

It shouldn't have been a problem, not even for a guy who had worked in the positions he had, but he was unique in that he barely knew who he was. His family life was as blank as a brand new notebook.

"Okay," James said, wondering how quickly he would run out of things to tell her.

"And I'm going to make it quantitative, so you'll have less wiggle room. Say, one new thing each week."

He was quickly going to run out of things to tell her.

"Also, every weekend I would get a certain time period, say . . . five hours, where the cameras are off in my apartment and I can have my friends and family over and not be watched."

"Not five hours," James said immediately. Five hours was way too long.

"I would be making a lot of compromises and you would have to, too," she said, leaning back into her chair.

"Three hours, max. And the cameras outside stay on," James said.

"Four," Mak said.

"Three and a half."

Mak stared at him. "Agreed. Three and a half."

"Three and a half, but if I'm out of town for work, the cameras stay on—no exceptions," James clarified.

"Understood," Mak said with a grin.

"Anything else?" James said.

"That's it . . . for now. But I'm still thinking this over, and even if I did agree, I would still reserve the right to renegotiate at any time."

James pushed his chair back and motioned for her to come over. She walked around the table and climbed onto his lap.

"Of course you could renegotiate at any time," James said, holding her waist. "You could change your mind at any time. You could walk away at any time. If you were to decide that this is not what you want, then we would part ways nicely and say goodbye. And I would fully understand."

She placed her hands on his chest and looked into his eyes.

He brought his mouth to hers, and Mak kissed him with the hunger he felt inside. He wanted her, more than he'd ever wanted another woman, but she still wasn't his—not yet.

He pulled back just as his phone vibrated in his pocket. He knew it was bad news before he even looked at the caller ID.

"Samuel," James said.

"You need to come downstairs now," Samuel said.

"Right now?"

"Right now, James."

James took a deep breath—he didn't want to leave, he didn't want to hear Samuel's bad news.

He put the phone down on the table. "Mak, I have to go and have a look at something urgent. And this is another thing we're going to have to contend with because my company sometimes deals with life-and-death situations. I don't know what is going on, but when I receive a call like that I have to drop everything. I need to go now, but I promise you I'll be back as soon as I can."

"Um, okay," she said, climbing off his lap.

"Stay here and help yourself to anything. You can watch television in my bedroom if you want," he said on his way out.

James took the stairs so quickly he felt like he was flying, but when he marched into Samuel's office he stopped dead in his tracks. He looked at the image on the screen and he felt like he'd been shot in the chest with two bullets.

It was Dasha. Both her hands had been cut off and her eyes gouged out. It wasn't the sight of her mutilated body but rather the piece of cloth nailed to her throat that made his heart stop. It was a piece of military uniform with a name tape.

A name he hadn't heard for so many years that it now seemed unfamiliar to him.

The first name he had ever known.

HART

Joshua Hart.

//

ALSO BY BROOKE SIVENDRA

THE JAMES THOMAS SERIES

#1 - ESCANTA

#2 - SARATANI

#3 - SARQUIS

#4 - LUCIAN

#5 - SORIN

#0.5 - THE FAVOR

The complete James Thomas series is available now. THE FAVOR is a novella, and Brooke recommends reading it after SORIN.

THE SOUL SERIES

#1 - The Secrets of Their Souls

#2 - The Ghosts of Their Pasts

#3 - The Blood of Their Sins

A GIFT FROM BROOKE

Brooke is giving away the first book of the Soul Series, *The Secrets of Their Souls*, for **FREE**. All you need to do is sign up here:

http://brookesivendra.com/tsots-download/

Enjoy!

DID YOU ENJOY THIS BOOK?

As a writer, it is critically important to get reviews.

Why?

You probably weigh reviews highly when making a decision whether to try a new author—I definitely do.

So, if you've enjoyed this book and would love to spread the word, I would be so grateful if you could leave an honest review (as short or as long as you like) where you bought it.

Thank you so much,
Brooke

ABOUT THE AUTHOR

Brooke Sivendra lives in Adelaide, Australia with her husband and two furry children—Milly, a Rhodesian Ridgeback, and Lara, a massive Great Dane who is fifty pounds heavier than Brooke and thinks she is a lap dog!

Brooke has a degree in Nuclear Medicine and worked in the field of medical research before launching her first business at the age of twenty-six. This business grew to be Australia's premier online shopping directory, and Brooke recently sold it to focus on her writing.

You can connect with Brooke at any of the channels listed below, and she personally responds to every comment and email.

Website: www.brookesivendra.com
Email: brooke@brookesivendra.com
Facebook: http://www.facebook.com/bsivendra
Instagram: http://www.instagram.com/brookesivendra
Twitter: www.twitter.com/brookesivendra

AUTHOR ACKNOWLEDGEMENTS

To my readers, who have taken this journey with me—thank you. Your support for The Soul Series has made this book possible, and I hope you loved ESCANTA. Thank you for your daily emails of encouragement and your heartfelt Facebook messages. I smile every single time I read them.

To my editor, Lorelei, thank you for your encouragement and your gentle criticism—both of which have made me into a much better writer.

To Jeya, there are a million things I want to thank you for, but most of all, thank you for your tireless support. I know it's not always easy being married to a dreamer.

Made in the USA
Lexington, KY
25 April 2018